HOW TO LOVE A COWBOY

COWBOY ROMANCE - BOOK 1

JESSA JAMES

GET A FREE BOOK!

Join my mailing list to be the first to know of new releases, free books, special prices and other author giveaways.

http://freehotcontemporary.com

How To Love A Cowboy:
Copyright © 2018 by Jessa James
ISBN: 978-1-7959-0203-8

All Rights Reserved. No part of this book may be reproduced or transmitted in any form or by any means, electrical, digital or mechanical including but not limited to photocopying, recording, scanning or by any type of data storage and retrieval system without express, written permission from the author.

Published by Jessa James
James, Jessa
How To Love A Cowboy

Cover design copyright 2018 by Jessa James, Author
Images/Photo Credit: Deposit Photos: aarrttuurr

Publisher's Note:

This book was written for an adult audience. The book may contain explicit sexual content. Sexual activities included in this book are strictly fantasies intended for adults and any activities or risks taken by fictional characters within the story are neither endorsed nor encouraged by the author or publisher.

This book has been previously published.

ABOUT HOW TO LOVE A COWBOY

Pete

The Killarny Estate is getting ready for the Waters Derby. I still remember little Sara Waters and how she'd grabbed and kissed me in the barn on the Waters property when she was 10 years old. The last time I'd seen her I'd been with my ex-wife, Kelly. The only good thing out of that marriage had been my 12-year-old daughter. I haven't had a solid relationship since.

When Sara shows up at the ranch to tell me that her dad isn't letting the Killarny's enter the derby, that we're doing

something illegal, well let's just say, I didn't take it very well. There's no way in hell we're not going, and no way in hell I can stay away from that hot, little body.

Sara

My father's instructions were clear – tell the Killarny's they can't race. Our families have history and I refuse to tell them over the phone, so I'll drive to the Estate to tell them in person. But Pete Killarny refuses to accept my dad's decision. Who am I supposed to believe: the father who's cared for me all my life or the hot cowboy I've loved since I was 10 years old?

If fantasies involving hay lofts give you a thrill, along with the thought of a family of HOT brothers, read on…

1

Pete

I closed the ledger and leaned back into the rich cherry colored leather of the desk chair. I closed my eyes and rubbed my temples, thinking about how much easier things had been when my father was around running things at Killarny Estate. It wasn't anything I hadn't become accustomed to over the years. Being the oldest of the five Killarny brothers, it was expected from birth that I would be the one to take over the day to day running of the ranch. While all the brothers were equal partners in running the ranch, it was I who was the most responsible. Ask anyone. It was also me that my dad had turned to back when my mother, Emily Killarny, had first been diagnosed with breast cancer.

At my mother's request, I took on the additional tasks that my father had usually taken care of. Most of it was business, the sort of thing that didn't capture my attention quite like the quiet, meditative work with the horses, but I knew what had to be done. Most of all, I hadn't wanted to let my mother down.

Emily Killarny was a force unto herself, but she had a kind and good heart, and above all, she loved her children. I was aware that I had a special place in her heart when she had gone out of her way to be the best kind of grandmother she could be to Emma. I'd been dejected and alone, raising a two year old daughter alone after my ex-wife, Kelly, decided one day that motherhood and married life wasn't for her. My parents had been so kind to us in the days following that abandonment, and I would forever be grateful to both of them. My mother had especially done all that she could to make sure that Emma felt safe and loved after her mother's abrupt departure.

Back then my major responsibilities had been tending to the horses, something I still loved and wished I was able to do more of, but being the oldest, and since my father had relocated to Costa Rica, I knew I had to be the one to step up to the plate. My mother's death three years prior had taken a toll on the family patriarch, and after suffering a severe bout of depression, he finally decided to make some major changes. One of those changes included leaving the states and relocating to a warmer climate, leaving the green Kentucky hills behind him in favor of sun and sand. Some days I couldn't help but feel a little jealous of that, but I knew that my heart would always be right here, wherever Emma was.

I opened my eyes again and looked at my computer screen for a moment before getting up and heading for the door, grabbing my jacket on the way. There was still a chill in the air that early in the Kentucky spring and it was invigorating to step out into the morning air, breathing in the fresh smell of new grass and the less pleasing scent wafting from the nearest barn. The smell of manure might not have appealed to everyone, but for me, it was a reminder of home and childhood.

I breathed in the air and made my way over to the stables where my brother Alex was brushing out the coat of a two year old mare.

"She looks beautiful," I said as I came up to stand on the other side of the stall door.

Alex nodded. "Siobhan is quite a looker." He brushed her russet coat to a glistening sheen that caught the early morning sun and made the horse look like a copper penny.

"You think we'll run her next year?" I asked him as I looked over the horse from nose to tail. She was beautiful, but I wasn't sure if she was one of the horses that we would end up taking to the many derbies we were involved in.

Alex shrugged. "Not sure. She hasn't been run that much, and I really think that if we had planned on doing that with her, she should have seen a little more practice at this point in her life. I think she is a great horse, but I'm not sure the derby life is the one for her. However, I do think she is going to give us a lot of talented foals."

Alex was probably the quietest of all the brothers, so hearing him talk this much was a little unusual. The only time Alex had much to say was when he was talking about a horse. Not much for words and usually keeping to himself, he was definitely the most horse whisperer like among us and was more involved with the training of individuals here at the ranch. He was so in tune with the horses that it helped to have his expertise around to help people become accustomed to green horses. While most of our horses were bred here on the ranch, we did keep a group of wild ponies from the Dakotas on one of the spreads of land that was fenced off from the rest. Alex's house was out there and visiting that part of the ranch felt like entering a wilderness. I could see why my parents had given him that parcel when they were divvying up the land to us. It fit my younger brother's personality perfectly, and he was never happier than he was when he was among the wild horses.

"Her mother is Spring, right?" I asked.

"Yeah, and her father was David's Lariat."

David's Lariat had been one of Alex's favorites. A horse that my father had acquired from a Colorado ranch when we were still very young, the horse had been a monster of an animal when we got him. He stood taller than any of our other horses but managed to be faster than almost any horse half his weight. He was a marvel and had produced many of our fastest horses. David's Lariat had died just a year before, but we still had a few of his offspring around the ranch and would likely see his influence in our derby horses for decades to come.

"Well, even if she isn't going to run for us, she's a beautiful girl, and I'm sure she'll give us a few great runners."

"What are you up to?" Alex asked as he put away the brush and stepped out of the stall to join me where I stood.

I shrugged. "Just needed to get out of the office for a little while."

"Already?" He looked at his watch. "It's early in the day. Why don't you hire someone to take care of some of the stuff you don't enjoy? That's what bookkeepers are for, after all. It would give you a break and let you have a chance to get back out here with the horses where you want to be."

Alex was perceptive with more than just the horses.

"Yeah, well, I might do that after the next couple of

derbies have passed. I've got too much on my plate right now to hand it over to someone totally new."

My brother sighed and shrugged. "Whatever you say. Just don't be afraid to ask for a little help when you need it."

I gave him a firm pat on the back and continued on down through the stables, past the stalls that housed our many horses. A few of our ranch hands were leading some of the horses out to graze in the pasture, while some of them were headed to the arena and our track for training. As I exited the other end of the massive stable, I saw Emma atop her horse, Saoirse.

"How'dya do, Miss Emma Lou?"

Emma frowned at me, and I could see her brow furrowing under her helmet. I knew she hated it when I referred to her middle name, Louise, but told myself that someday she would come to think of it as endearing, so I kept up the practice.

She tossed her head back. "Saoirse and I just went out for our morning run. I was about to take her back to the stable and then head in for my lessons. Is Hetty here yet?"

I shook my head. "She wasn't there when I left the house, but there's a good chance she's arrived by now. Better hurry on back, you don't want to be late."

My twelve year old daughter beamed at me from where she sat on her horse and headed into the stable before dismounting. I watched her lead her young horse into the stall and couldn't help but notice how much she was starting to look like her mother. It wasn't a bad thing, but I did wonder how Emma would feel as she looked in the mirror and started to notice the resemblance she shared with the woman who left her—and me—behind when Emma was just a toddler.

I walked toward the pasture as I recalled the time

directly after Kelly left. It had been a shock to me when it happened, but when I had a little time to think it over, nothing about it was too surprising. We had married straight out of high school, and my parents had been opposed to the match from the start. Kelly's parents were business owners in the nearest town, and ours had been the kind of wedding that made the local papers. Our courtship had been brief — we dated at the end of high school, and because I was an idiot, I had proposed to Kelly not long after graduation. We married and moved into a house here at Killarny Estate and had had a hell of a time for the first couple of years.

Kelly was wild and looking back I could tell she had been just a little too wild for me. It wasn't something I had noticed at the time, and while it was just the two of us, it was easy to forget that we were stepping into a new world that included all sorts of new responsibilities. Back then we would spend our weekends hopping around the bars in town before heading back to the privacy of our house at the ranch and going at it like rabbits. It was no surprise when Kelly got pregnant, and I was overjoyed, but she didn't seem too enthused about it. Slowly she warmed to the idea, and once Emma was born, I could see that she really did love our daughter.

Things were never the same though. Kelly never looked at me the same way, and I tried to encourage her to go see a doctor to see if what she was struggling with was postpartum depression, but she wouldn't listen.

I came home one evening to find all of Kelly's things gone, a note on the kitchen table, and Emma wailing in her playpen. I had picked up my daughter and the note and read the words through tears as Emma sniffled and buried her head against my shoulder. Kelly was gone. She apologized in the letter, said she was heading to California to pursue her dream of being an actress, and that she was going with her friend, Bud.

Bud was the guy she had dated before me in high school, and suddenly it all started to make sense. We never really heard from her after that, aside from a Christmas card or a birthday present for Emma on the years that Kelly remembered, which were few and far between.

As far as I knew, Emma had no real memory of her mother. It made me sad, but I wondered if it was for the best that she didn't know what she was missing out on. If Kelly had hung around much longer, it would have been more difficult than it already was to get Emma used to not having her mother around.

I had been so grateful to my parents for the support they were during that time, especially my mother. She had done all she could to be the maternal figure in my daughter's life, but she never stopped pressing me to go on dates and get out there again, constantly reminding me that I was still young and there was happiness out there for me if I would just go looking for it.

Her last attempt had been just a few years before she passed away when I had first hired Hetty Blackburn, a local teacher, to be Emma's tutor. The ranch was well out of the way, and it was quite a hike to the nearest school, so I had decided to homeschool Emma. It gave her a chance to be around the horses more and to study at her own pace, which was quite a bit faster than the average elementary school student, according to Hetty.

Hetty was pretty and a very sweet woman. Her black hair and blue eyes were a sort of bewitching combination that was hard to ignore, but I couldn't get back into dating; not then and not now, even though it was 10 years since Kelly walked out. Even if I hadn't already been very hesitant to date, Hetty already had one major strike against her—she knew my daughter.

I leaned against the bright white fence and watched as a group of our horses played together in the dewy field that was filled with clover. The place was even more picturesque than usual in this light. Killarny Estate was really something to be proud of, and I was so glad to have the privilege of being a part of a four generation horse ranch, the largest one in Kentucky, and now, for all intents and purposes, running the place.

One rule I had established for myself was that until I knew I could trust a woman, she would never meet my daughter. And since I wasn't in the mood to start dating yet, nothing had ever made it that far. Sure, I had been with women since Kelly—too many to count—but I was there to get what I wanted and get out. I never went out with anyone that I thought was there for more than what I was because I had more heart than that. But I didn't trust anyone to give me any more than what I was looking for at the moment. It was sex, pure and simple—though rarely pure or simple. I was there for a release, to have sex, hear them scream my name, and then leave quietly. The closest I had ever come to bringing a woman home was the Lawrence girl who I made it all the way back to the ranch with, but we never left my truck. We had made it as far as the pecan grove when I pulled over and had her right there in the cab of my pickup. When we were done, I turned around and drove her right back to her house. But that had been the last one, and that had been a long time ago now.

There was no need to complicate my life any more than it already was and I was certainly not going to bring any of these women into the life of my daughter. She had already experienced enough pain from my poor choices, and I wasn't going to do that to her again.

My middle brother, Jake, came riding up on his stallion and brought the horse to a quick halt a few feet away from me.

"Showing off?" I asked as I cocked my eyebrow at him.

He swung down off the saddle and gave the horse a pat. "This bastard is ready to run!"

Clement certainly looked like he was ready for it. His eyes were wild, but it was clear that he was happy after his morning run with Jake.

"Think about how fast he's going to be with one of the jockeys on him!"

I nodded. "We're taking him to the Waters derby, right?"

"Yup, just a couple of weeks away now."

I noted to myself that I needed to check that out on the calendar. There was still a lot left to do in preparation, and we weren't sure how many horses we would be taking. Clement was certainly on the top of the list, but I knew we needed to have a few backups. Killarny Estate had always been top of the pack as far as producing some of the fastest race horses in the country, but ever since my father had packed it up and gone to Costa Rica, it felt like we had lost some of our edge. I had no idea what it was Dad had that we didn't quite have down yet, other than the forty years of experience. What I did know was that it was crucial for us to win this derby. Things were tight, and if we were going to turn them around and maintain things the way they were around here, or if we were ever going to have any hope of making Killarny the very best again, we had to win the Waters derby.

"You coming?" Jake asked me as he brushed his reddish-brown hair back out of his face and wiped his brow with the back of his sleeve.

I looked at him bewildered. "Of course I am."

He shrugged. "Don't act like it's a given. You haven't been there in years."

"Yeah, well...now I don't really have any choice, do I? Dad is still in Costa Rica, and I don't know the next time he's planning on coming back, so I've got to be there to represent the ranch. And I think Emma would enjoy the trip to Tennessee, so yeah, I'll be there."

"You're not nervous, are you?" Jake winked at me, and I frowned in response.

"Why would I be nervous?"

"Because," he began, pausing to spit on the ground. "Little Sara Waters is going to be there. I wonder if she is going to follow you around like she always used to when we were kids."

I rolled my eyes. "Sara Waters is thirty by now. I am sure she has got better things to do than chase around a nearly middle-aged man with his twelve year old daughter in tow."

"Hey now, don't write yourself off just yet. You're only a year or so older than her, right? I bet she would be champing at the bit to get a piece of a Killarny brother."

I shook my head and started off back toward the stable, Jake following behind me with Clement.

"Then she can have her pick of the other four. Hell, she can have both Stephen and Sam if she wants them." I stopped and looked around. "Speaking of that, where are the twins?"

Jake shrugged as he continued toward the stable. "Who the hell knows. They're out every night of the week. Probably still in bed."

I knew he was kidding about the last thing. If we had

been taught anything as kids, it was that getting up early in the morning was the Killarny way.

"Okay, well. I need to go find them. I'll get back to you about the Waters derby. We need to talk about some logistics getting there, but it can wait until later."

As I walked off toward the other barns to locate my two youngest brothers, I couldn't help thinking about what Jake had said regarding Sara Waters. I hadn't seen her since we were practically teenagers. It must have been a decade or so. I wondered what she looked like now and if there was a chance that we'd get some time alone when I was at her father's derby in a few weeks.

2

Sara

"Sara?"

I looked up from the top of my reading glasses that I used only when I was working on my laptop. They were sliding down my nose, and I pulled them off my face and rubbed the bridge of my nose as I looked at Elsie, my father's secretary, standing in the doorway of my office.

"Yes?"

"Your father would like to see you. He said he's got a few last minute things to go over for the derby."

Of course, he does, I thought as I flashed Elsie a smile and a nod. He was waiting until two weeks before our derby to go over something that I had a feeling would be of utmost importance and require my immediate attention. It was the typical stunt my father always pulled this time of year.

"I'll be right there. I'm just finishing up a few things."

My father acted as if his office wasn't right down the hall

from mine. He certainly could have used what little exercise the walk would have provided, but I knew he was never in any kind of temperament to hear my suggestion.

I closed my laptop and grabbed my notebook full of notes for the upcoming derby and headed down the hallway to his office. I found my father leaning back in his chair, grinning wide, with a cigar hanging out of his mouth as he chuckled into his phone.

"Well, well. How about that! I imagine we'll be seeing her here in a couple of years then. That's great, Jameson. I look forward to seeing you in a few weeks. I'll talk to you later." He snapped the flip phone shut, and I shook my head, still surprised that the man refused to upgrade his cell phone from the one he had gotten ten years prior.

"That thing is going to give out on you," I said with a half-smile.

"Nah, she's holding up. They don't make things like they used to. I'll use her until it's time to put her out to pasture." He tapped the end of his cigar on the ashtray on his desk.

"You know, I could probably call OSHA about you smoking in here. I'm sure they'd have something to say about your daily cigar and the fact that your most valuable employee has to be exposed to carcinogens."

He laughed. "Sweetheart, that's the beauty of a home office. I'm the king around here. What I say, goes."

"And your lungs may as well," I said as I scrunched my nose and waved the smoke out of the air. "Elsie said you had a few things to talk to me about."

He cleared his throat and put the cigar down in the ashtray, a thin thread of smoke rising from the tip.

"I sure do. With the derby coming up we've got a lot going on, and I know you've been just as busy as I have."

I smirked but didn't say anything. The idea that my

father had been doing as much work around here for the derby as I had was laughable. Beyond making phone calls to his good ol' boys at ranches around the country, he didn't do an awful lot for the derby anymore. Most of the work was left to the rest of us and since I was second in charge most of it fell on my lap to take care of.

"It is definitely the busiest time of year for us," I said with a nod.

He narrowed his eyes, and I could tell the wheels in his brain were turning.

"I hate to ask you to do much more, but I need you to make a call and take care of something for me."

"What is it?" I asked, leaning in to see what he was looking at on his desk. He pushed a folder toward me. It was labeled 'Killarny Estate'.'

"What's going on with the Killarnys?"

My father took a deep breath. "I'm going to need you to tell them they won't be entering a horse in this year's derby. Not this one and, not the next one. Not ever again."

I looked at him with my mouth agape. "Why would you remove the Killarnys from the derby? They've had a relationship with us for as long as anyone has and they have been a very valuable draw for us. People come from all over to see who the Killarnys are racing. Dad...you're going to have to explain."

"I've got my reasons," he said, sounding suspicious as he picked up the cigar again.

I crossed my arms in front of my chest and leaned back into my chair. "Well, you're going to have to tell me what they are before I go about ending one of the oldest relationships we have with a stable. Aren't you considering the kind of repercussions this could have?"

He shrugged. "Listen to me, Sara. There's more going on

here than what you think you know. I've been suspecting them of some things for quite some time, and I just want to keep things above board around here."

"Above board?" I was confused. I had only ever known the Killarny Estate horses to be absolutely clean thoroughbreds. I couldn't imagine the family being involved in something unsavory. "What are they doing? Are they colluding with someone? Fixing a race?" It was the only thing I could think of, but it seemed very far off base. Anything else though...would be nearly criminal to consider.

"I think they are doping their horses." He said the words matter of factly and waited for me to respond.

"You're kidding, right? Jesus, Dad, you've known Sean Killarny forever. The last thing they would do is dope their horses."

"People do it all the time. You know that. When the testing isn't as rigorous, it's especially bad! And I've been noticing a few things over the years that have left me very suspicious of them. I also think that they've been using this relationship for a long time now and think that they can get away with it. Well, I've got news for Sean Killarny—it's done. I don't mess with dopers, and I won't have them giving my derby a bad name. Imagine if the word got out that this was going on. People would bring this relationship up in the discussion for sure and then you would have folks looking at our derby. Think about all the sponsorship we could lose, not to mention our license." He took a deep breath. "No, I cannot allow it to continue. They can't keep coming here if they are going to operate that way."

My mind was whirling, trying to put all the pieces together. I couldn't believe that my father really thought the Killarnys were drugging their horses, but he was right—

some people did, and if we were accused of having any connection to them it could look very bad for us.

"Evidence...I'm going to need to see something. I can't just call them up and tell them without—"

"Sara." He cut me off and held up his hand to silence me. "Trust me. I know what is going on over there. We can have no connection to it. I can make the call if you would rather not take care of this yourself, but since you are in charge of day to day operations, I thought it would be best if you took care of this yourself. If you can't though..." he reached for his phone.

I shook my head. "No, I'll take care of it. But I don't think this is something I can do over the phone. I mean...Dad, they already paid the registration fee. We're going to have to give that back to them if you don't want any trouble out of this. They could sue you."

He laughed. "There's no way they are suing me. I know what they are up to and they sure as hell know what's going on underneath the roof of their stables. Neither Sean nor his boys have the balls to take me to court because they know they are the ones who will end up in hot water if they do that." My father opened one of his desk drawers and pulled out a checkbook. He picked up his pen and began making out the check, complete with the required number of zeroes. He signed his name and thrust the check at me. "Here, take it. Put it in the mail."

I sighed. "Unfortunately, I think this is the sort of thing that has to be done in person. You know, we want to finesse this and treat it as sensitively as possible. They were our friends for a long time, and no matter what they are up to now, it would be inappropriate to put an end to a decade long relationship over the phone. I'll take tomorrow off and drive up there to deliver this myself. Then maybe there won't be much animosity."

I got up and headed back to my office, trying to think how I could possibly smooth this over with the Killarnys. If my father was right then, we did need to end the relationship, but I definitely didn't want to call them out on doping their horses without any evidence. No, I was going to have to cancel their registration and chalk it up as some kind of a mistake on our end. I would deal with it next year when it rolled around. Maybe their registration could get lost in the mail or something, but I would deal with that when it happened. Right now I needed to focus on how I was going to get them to believe whatever I said. And I needed to do it in a way that didn't look completely suspicious.

Picking up my phone I looked up the number for Killarny Estate and dialed. A woman picked up, and I gave her my name.

"Mr. Killarny isn't in right now. Could I take a message?"

Of course, a message. But what on earth would Sean Killarny believe?

"Could you tell him it's Sara Waters and I'm just checking on some derby business? I'll be by tomorrow afternoon if that's okay. I wanted a chance to speak to him in person."

"Okay then...it looks like he's got an open afternoon. If you ring the bell at the main house when you get here, then we'll find him for you. See you tomorrow, Miss Waters."

I left the next morning and made the three hour drive to the Killarny Estate. It was nestled in an area with rolling green hills and was the most picturesque kind of horse ranch you could imagine. I knew I was getting close when I saw the pristine white fencing, but I was still several miles from the main entrance to the ranch. As soon as I pulled up to the stone arch, memories came flooding back of the time I spent here when I was a child. On occasion when my father purchased a horse from the Killarnys or had some derby business with them we would come up for a day visit, and I spent most of the time tormenting Pete Killarny, the oldest of the brothers who was the closest to my age. And to my ten year old eyes, he was the cutest. Back then he had sandy blond hair, blue eyes, and a few freckles dappled across his nose. I wasn't quite as cute at the time. A little on the chubby side, my hair was frizzy, and I was just about to get braces. Soon after the glasses followed and it didn't surprise me that when I had made Pete Killarny my first kiss he had been very reluctant.

I cringed at that particular memory and hoped that I wouldn't run into him here. Of course, it had been years since that had happened and we had seen each other several times since then, but it didn't change the fact that it was one of the most embarrassing moments of my entire life. Pete had looked at me incredulously and somewhat shocked, then turned around and left the old barn where the kiss had occurred. It was while they had been visiting Tennessee for our derby and now that I thought about it, it must have been exactly twenty years prior. So much time had passed. I eventually grew up and out of my braces, glasses, and baby fat, and Pete had grown into a very attractive young man. The last time I saw him, he was dating a new girl, and I remember how she had clung to him like a leech from a pond on a hot summer day.

It surprised me to remember how jealous I had been at that moment. The girl was unknown to me, but I hated seeing Pete with another girl, no matter how ga-ga they appeared to be over each other. She had been drop dead gorgeous, and there was no way I could hold a candle to her black hair and blue eyes. She had been thin as a rail and just looked the part of a girl who would end up marrying the heir to a massive horse ranch.

"God, maybe I'll run into her again, too," I said as I pulled into the circle drive in front of the main house. It was a gorgeous white colonial with massive pillars and a lamp that hung down in front of the front door. The place was positively palatial, and I was sure there had to have been many renovations since the last time I had stepped foot in the house.

I hopped out of my SUV and made my way to the front door where I rang the bell that let out the longest chime in the history of doorbells, and I waited for someone to answer. A middle-aged woman came to the door with a smile on her face.

"Can I help you?" she asked.

I smiled back at her. "I'm here for a meeting with Mr. Killarny. I called and spoke with his secretary yesterday."

She nodded. "Come right in. I'll show you to his office."

The woman led me from the main foyer with it's wide staircase that was appropriate for a royal presentation, down a hallway that led to an even smaller hallway. She opened the first door and ushered me inside.

"I'll see that Pete knows you're here," she said as she closed the door behind her and before I could say anything she was gone.

I looked around in surprise. The nameplate on the desk said it plain as day. Pete Killarny. Where was Sean? Maybe the man didn't have time for me, and he was letting one of his sons take care of the business today. Thoughts ran through my mind, and I tried to calm myself down. It wasn't a big deal that I had to deal with Pete. He was probably just as knowledgeable about the ranch business as his father was. After all, what was I doing here? Taking care of things for my father.

And it wasn't as if Pete and I had a history beyond me kissing him once when I was a child. There was some kind of electric tension in the air though at the thought of seeing him again. It was a little like when I had gone back to my ten year high school reunion. Of course, that had been a bust because of social media and the fact that I still lived in the same town where I had graduated from, but this meeting held the same kind of nervousness for me.

I wondered what he looked like and I glanced around the office to see if there was any sign of a photo. The walls were covered with bookshelves which were filled with hardback, leather-bound volumes. It looked like mostly classics or the sort of thing you could get an interior decorator to put together for you. I wasn't sure if Pete was much of a reader, but he had never struck me as one. When we were young, he had been the jock, the kind of guy other guys wanted to be, and all the girls wanted to be with. He was less obvious about it than some guys were though and really seemed to have a sweet and genuine side if you could get past the hard exterior.

A quick sweep of the room revealed nothing, and there was no sign of any photos on his desk. I thought it was peculiar, but it also didn't look like it was Pete's office for some reason.

I waited and watched the grandfather clock tick until several minutes had passed and then I heard the doorknob rattle. When I turned I saw that another woman was standing there, this one much younger and looking a little uncertain.

"Miss Waters?"

"Yes, I was just waiting for Mr. Killarny...but I thought I was going to be seeing Sean today."

Understanding swept over her facial features. "Oh, I'm sorry about that. I thought you knew that Pete was running the day to day operations now. But about that, I think he must have missed your name in his schedule for the day, and I'm afraid he is somewhere out on the property. Probably working with the horses. If you'd like me to try to call him, I could do that..."

I stood and shook my head. "No, there's no need for you to bother with that. I'm familiar with the place. If you don't mind, I'll just head out for a little stroll and see if I can find him."

She smiled at me and nodded. "By all means."

I made my way outside and down one of the pathways that led to the main stable and barns. The property was massive and meant he could be anywhere, so it might have been a foolish move not to have her call him. I had time to take a self-guided walking tour of Killarny Estate though.

Suddenly the reason I was here came back to me. If my dad thought they were doping their horses, then this might not be the wholesome family run ranch I had always thought it was. But I had no way of knowing and I wasn't sure that I wanted to go all out believing my dad's hunches at this point. Still, it wasn't going to be a pretty scene giving the check back to Pete, especially since he wasn't expecting it.

I entered the stable and found it empty other than several horses in their stalls. They were all calmly chewing on hay and barely looked up to regard me. I smiled as I walked down the middle of the stable, taking in the beauty of the animals that the Killarny family had bred and raised. They had some of the best thoroughbreds in the country, and people paid top dollar to get their hands on some of the horses that came from this ranch. Being up close and personal with the amazing animals was a real treat that I savored. I couldn't help having a love of horses. It had been instilled in me from a young age and even after my parents' divorce when I was very young, my mom had made sure that I spent equal time with my father, so I had been exposed to the horses from the time I could walk.

I stopped in front of one of the stalls and read the nameplate.

"Hello, Saoirse. These Killarnys like their Irish names, don't they? Well, you're a beautiful girl, there's no mistaking that."

"Can I help you?" The voice echoed from the other end of the stable, and I turned to see who it was. The light coming from the stable exit left the person standing there in silhouette, and I couldn't make out who it was until he got a little closer.

Pete Killarny. He wasn't the little boy I had kissed, but he wasn't much different from the young man I had last seen a little over ten years prior. His hair was darker now, and the freckles were gone, but his eyes were every bit as deep blue as they had been then. He had broadened though. His shoulders were wider, and he was muscular, a little bulkier than he had been when he was a teenager. No longer wiry, he walked with the confidence of a guy who owned the place.

And that he did. At least a portion of it.

But the part that surprised me, the most shocking feeling that I hadn't expected at all, was the immediate desire to jump him. He was incredibly handsome, and while that in itself wasn't a surprise, my reaction to him really was. Inside I was telling myself to calm down and that this wasn't the rational response to have when meeting someone you haven't seen in several years. And then there was the other thing...the thing I didn't want to think about but really needed to confront before I thought about tackling this guy and begging him to take me right there in the stable.

I was reacting this way because I needed this. It had been a year since I'd walked in on my fiancé Dalton sleeping with my best friend, Meg, and called it all off. The big society wedding, the marriage that was going to make the kind of connections my father wanted me to have. I let it all go in that moment when I discovered the worst betrayal of my life.

And I hadn't had sex since. It had been a year since I had been with anyone. I knew because the date that was supposed to be our anniversary was coming up. And the day that I found Dalton with Meg, he had been with me earlier in the day. That morning before he left for work we had made love and talked about our plans for dinner that night, but I had come home to pick up something I had forgotten and walked in on the two of them together. It had ruined everything, and I tried not to think about it any more often than I had to.

But here I was, in front of Pete Killarny, thinking about how badly I wanted to know what he looked like naked.

"Hi Pete...it's been a long time." I laughed, but it was clear he had no clue who I was. "It's Sara...Sara Waters."

3

Pete

When I entered the stable and saw the woman standing in front of Saoirse I couldn't tell who she was. Obscured by the light coming from the entrance at the other end of the stable, all I could see was that she had one hell of a body and I wanted to get a better look.

When she turned and smiled at me, there was a glimmer of recognition in her eye, but I struggled to think when I had ever met this beautiful woman. And then she said her name.

"What the hell are you doing here?" I asked, hardly realizing what I was saying.

She looked taken aback. "Well, it's good to see you too, but that's not any way to greet someone you haven't seen in more than a decade."

I cleared my throat. "I...uh, sorry about that. You just

took me by surprise. I wasn't expecting to see you standing here in the middle of my stable."

"I called and made an appointment," she frowned, "but you weren't there for our meeting."

I let out a breath and ran a hand through my hair. "Sorry about that. I'm still not used to checking the damn calendar every day. They've got a thing set up on my laptop but I'm not used to looking at it yet, and frankly, I'm pretty annoyed that some damn alarm keeps going off every day. Haven't figured out how to fix that yet, but I'll have someone get to it sometime." I made a mental note to ask Emma. Of course, my twelve year old daughter would know exactly how to make the alarm stop bugging me.

But what was Sara Waters doing here? It didn't make any sense to find her here in the middle of the stable, standing in front of Emma's horse's stall. I was still shocked at the sight of her. This was not the girl who had pestered me and followed me around everywhere I went when we were kids.

She was smiling at me, and I finally smiled back. "So, when was the last time I saw you?"

She crossed her arms and leaned against one of the stall doors. "Well, it was a little over ten years ago. And I think it was here for some event. I saw you, but we didn't speak. You had a girl with you, and I think were talking about getting married sometime after that."

I nodded, realizing exactly when she must have seen me last. "Ah, right. Yeah, that was Kelly. We got married."

"Is she here? Can I meet her?" Sara looked genuinely interested.

I shook my head and held up my bare left hand. "We're not married anymore."

"Oh, that's a shame. I guess? Or maybe you're happier?"

I shrugged. "You know how it goes. Relationships come and go, and Kelly was gone from my life about as quickly as she entered it. She did give me a beautiful daughter though, and I'll always be grateful for that. Other than that though… yeah, for the past twelve years I've been here, working on the ranch, raising my daughter, and just living."

"Wow, well, it sounds like you've been a busy guy."

"What about you?" I didn't remember seeing her the last time she was here, and she had changed so much it was hard to believe this was the same, Sara.

She tossed her dark brown hair over her shoulder, and I admired the deep brown of her eyes, accentuated with her dark black lashes.

"I went to college and did all of that. Came back home to help my dad out and I've been doing that ever since. Got engaged for a little while, but that didn't work out." She shrugged, but I could see something in her eyes when she said that. It was clear the topic was off limits just from her body language, and I was surprised she had brought it up at all.

"Well, it is good to see you again."

She tilted her head at me and asked, "Why didn't you ever come to any of the derbies? I would have known if you were there. Too busy back here?"

I thought about it for a moment. It wasn't that there was something keeping me away from the Waters derby, not really. There had been a shadow hanging over that part of my life for some time, and I didn't want to bring it up with Sara. We weren't close at all, but the truth was that I had thought about her often over the years as the family name was brought up. Some part of me didn't want to go there and face her father or her. So much of what had happened with Kelly had left me reeling, and I had stuck around the ranch, never venturing far. I liked my work here, and if they didn't need me at the derby, then I didn't go. That's why God gave me four brothers' as far as I was concerned.

"Things come up. You know. But I was planning on being at the upcoming derby, as a matter of fact."

She seemed to grimace somewhat, but I wasn't sure why.

"Would you like to go to my office and talk?"

Sara hesitated but started walking back toward the stable entrance with me. "We probably don't have to go back there. We can just talk out here in the open if that's okay with you."

I gave her a look. "Is everything okay?" I hadn't seen her in a long time, but I didn't have to be an expert to know that she looked like a woman who had something to say that she didn't particularly want to.

She sighed and stopped there in the stable, and I turned to face her again.

"The truth is that everything isn't okay and I've got some bad news to share with you." Sara was looking from side to side, maybe to check if there was anyone else around.

"Tell me. What is it?"

She looked seriously troubled to be telling me whatever it was and I couldn't imagine where she was going with this. Maybe her father was ill? Or the derby was going under?

"You're not going to be able to run any horses this year."

The words didn't register at first. I tried to make sense of them, but how could she be serious? There had been a Killarny Estate horse in their derby for as long as it had been going. And this was the biggest one of the year. She couldn't possibly expect us to sit this one out.

"You're going to have to explain to me because I am completely at a loss as to why you could be asking us to sit this one out," I said plainly.

She sighed and rolled her eyes. "Listen, Pete. I don't want to do this, and I don't really want to get into the middle of anything that is going on around here, but my father has some concerns, and we think it best that you guys are not a part of our event this year. I would really rather not get into details. I don't want to offend you or your operation." She pulled a check out of her purse and stuck her hand out toward me. "Here...it's the full amount you paid for registration. Every bit of it. We don't expect you to pay for a race you aren't going to run in. Please take it and know that it's with my deepest regrets that we have to do this."

I narrowed my eyes at her. "You have to do this? Why, because your father told you to?"

She braced herself and thrust her chin forward defiantly. "I am acting in the best interests of my family's company. This is the way it has to be, and if you have a problem with it well, I'm the one you have to talk to so let's hash it out here."

I chuckled and looked down at the check in her hand. "Honestly, Ron Waters sends his little girl out here to take care of his business? What a fucking joke."

"I am no little girl," she retorted and for a moment I was struck by the way she said the words. This was no little girl at all. She was a woman and while I'd been attracted to her just a few moments before, now that she was acting like she had some kind of power...I had to admit that it was turning me on. But there was no way I would let her think she was getting the better of me.

"Why doesn't your dad just grow a pair and deal with this like a man. Do you know what this is about?"

Sara nodded her head, but I had serious doubts if she had any clue about the bad blood that he been brewing between our fathers over the past few decades.

I shook my head. "Bullshit! And I'm going to bet that

when you asked your daddy to explain himself, he came up with some bullshit reason about why we can't race. Maybe he even accused us of breaking the law. That sounds like some shit your dad would pull. Well, Sara, you can take that check back to where it came from and tell your daddy to shove it up his ass. We're not taking that money. Killarny is better than that, and we've got a contract for this derby. If you are going to keep us from showing up you're going to have to get a lawyer and then your dad is going to have to come up with a damn good reason, one that he can actually back up, before he's going to be able to keep us from running in that derby."

I hoped that my stern tone would be enough to get her to back off, but she was like a dog on a bone, and she wasn't going to let go.

"We'll call the sheriff on you. We won't let you on the property. If my father says you've done something that disqualifies you from being a part of the derby, then I trust him, and you're not going to be there." She reached out and grabbed my hand and thrust the check into my palm, but before she backed away, I grabbed her and pulled her toward me.

"What the hell!?" she exclaimed as I pulled her close to me. Our bodies pressed together, and I felt like I was on fire, every inch of my skin spontaneously combusting just from being so near to her. I couldn't explain the effect she was having on me, but I didn't want it to stop.

"Just who the hell do you think you are?" I growled, my voice was low and deep. "Who do you think you are showing up at my ranch, walking into my stable, and threatening me? You believe your daddy? Well, you better believe this: it's your daddy that's got a problem. You want to know what it is...you can ask him yourself. That's his business. But don't you think for a fucking minute you can walk in here making demands of me, waving a check in my face like that's going to make decades of racing in that derby go away."

Sara's eyes were like daggers, and I braced myself for a moment because I really thought she might spit in my face. She should just try it, I thought. See what that would get her.

"Listen, Pete..." she squirmed against me and I held her tighter, hoping that no one would come in and disturb this incredibly strange, but pleasing moment. I knew that from the outside looking in it would appear sketchy as hell. "I'm not trying to start some kind of beef with you. You just need to take the money and walk away. There won't be anymore trouble. I'm not one to cause any problems that are unwarranted, but my father has instructed me that you aren't racing. I'm telling you that if you show up in two weeks, there will be sheriffs there and they will escort you from the property."

I leaned in so our faces were just centimeters apart. I wanted to kiss her right there, but that would be too easy. No, this would come to me in time, but right now I was going to let it go.

"I dare him," I said as I released her and turned to walk toward the house.

I clinched my fists as I walked and I didn't turn around to see what she was doing. She still had that check, and that was all that mattered. If she tried to leave it with my secretary or in the mailbox, then the thing would be right back in the mail to her father. We weren't taking that money back. We would be at the derby. Come hell or high water, we would be there, and there wasn't a fucking thing she could do to stop us.

This all came down to the shit that was between my father and her father. It was something that no one talked about, and I refused to let my mind dwell on the details of it, but what I was firmly convinced of was that this was business to be handled between two men and not in the way that Ken Waters was trying to do it. This was the coward's way out to try and slam it all on us like we had anything to do with what happened all those years ago between my father and him.

The screen door slammed behind me as I entered through the back of the house and went into the kitchen. Emma was sitting at the kitchen table eating a snack and working on some homework. It was the sight of her that made me shift from the anger I had felt in front of Sara. I never wanted my daughter to see me that way, no matter how much what Sara said had stirred up inside me. For Emma, I was a rock and a place she could turn to whenever she worried about something. I never wanted her to be afraid to come to me, no matter what her problem was.

"Hey sweetie," I said, my tone instantly softening. I felt my pulse slow somewhat and I went to the refrigerator to get myself a glass of water. What I wanted after that showdown in the stable was a shot of whiskey, but I would wait until later for that.

"Hey, Dad. What's happening? Who was that lady here to see you? Amy said you had a business meeting with someone."

I waved my hand in the air nonchalantly as I took a big gulp of water, then wiped my mouth on the back of my hand.

"Somebody I used to know," I said.

Emma gave me a sly look. "Somebody you used to date."

I almost choked on my water. "Absolutely not."

"Why not?" Emma asked. She was always asking questions and lately it had turned to dating. I didn't know if it was something she was reading or watching on TV, but the girl had decided recently that because I didn't date that it was a problem she needed to fix.

I shook my head. "We knew each other when we were your age. We didn't date though. She wasn't really my type." I thought about what Sara had looked like when we were kids and remembered that goofy grin of hers which was endearing even after she got the braces.

"But you're grown ups now. Is she still not your type?"

"This conversation might be getting a little above your pay grade. What do you have going on over here in the way of homework?"

She frowned and turned the textbook toward me. "Hetty has me working on pre-algebra. It's not that bad, but there are a lot of 'x's in here to figure out."

"Exes have always given me problems," I said as I looked at the work on her notebook paper. "Dang girl, I don't think I was doing this kind of math until I was in 9th grade or so. How did you end up so smart?"

She shrugged. "I'm still trying to figure that one out. Uncle Alex says it doesn't have a d-a-m-n thing to do with you."

I laughed at that. "Thank you for not cursing. And your Uncle Alex may be right for once in his life. I'm going to my office to work on some things. You call me if you need help with anything, all right?"

Emma nodded, and I kissed her on top of her head before I headed off toward my office where I could be in the silence with my thoughts.

It wasn't silent for long because just as I sat down to check out the calendar and see exactly what we were risking if we didn't show up at the Waters derby, there was a crash of thunder and then the inevitable downpour began. It was spring in the south, and this was the expected forecast, so I wasn't entirely surprised. What I didn't anticipate was the door bell ringing and who would be on the other side of it.

4

Sara

"Start, dammit!" I urged my car as I turned the key in the ignition once more. It was no use. The thing was dead, and I was probably flooding the engine at this rate. I had made it a full mile down the long drive that led to the main house at Killarny Estate when my SUV decided it was done for the day. It seemed very unlikely that it would be able to make the three hour trip home if it couldn't even make it out of the driveway.

"You piece of shit." It wasn't a piece of shit though. It was only a few years old, and it had been pretty expensive. It was the car I had decided to get myself not long after Dalton, and I got engaged. We had been dating for several years at the time and were already talking about children, so it had only seemed appropriate that when it came time for me to get a new car, I would get one that would be good for towing around a family.

Since all of those plans had gone down the drain the purchase seemed a little ridiculous, but I had been happy with the car, and I had it, so I was grateful. But now here I was sitting barely a mile from the Killarny house, on Killarny property, with my car refusing to budge. It was literally one of the last places on the planet I wanted to be right now, and I had to be broken down.

I picked up my phone and dialed for roadside assistance. It would take them two hours to get out there, but by then it would be past their general business hours, and they couldn't get me a tow until the next morning. I hung up the phone thinking it must be a busy day for broken down cars and I got out of my vehicle. Standing there beside it for a few minutes I looked up toward the house and then back down the driveway again. It was another ten miles into the nearest town and while I was sure they had a tow service and a place I could stay, I had no idea what the phone number for a garage was and my cell service was so spotty that it was pointless to even try getting the search feature to work on my phone.

No, I had one single option left, and that was to turn around and walk back up the hill to the Killarny house and ask if I could use their phone to call for help.

"This is the universe's way of making you swallow your pride," I said to myself as I began walking back up the hill, the house in view the entire time. It was like the house was there, mocking me as I trudged back up toward it, reminding me that Pete Killarny was somewhere inside and the ridiculous man was bound and determined to stick it to me about the derby.

You wish, I thought, and a part of me really did think that the guy had some interest in me, but I was pretty sure it was nothing beyond the pure physicality of the moment. He was hotter than hell as he aged and it had been so long since I had been with anyone, of course, he held some kind of very basic sexual appeal for me. But I was not going to give into that. No, I was much more than the pure animal instinct that made me want to reach out and grab him. When he had pulled me close, I was nearly certain that he was going to close the gap and kiss me and I wished he would have. I remembered that first kiss like it was yesterday. It had been stolen, and he had looked so upset by it like he was surprised and then disappointed. Which he must have been given my awkward little girl state. There was nothing cute about being kissed by a girl your age when you were ten or so. Honestly, he probably wasn't even interested in girls at the time. I was sure I was keeping him from running off and playing with his brothers, and I remembered how much I used to pester the kid by running after him and begging him to play with me.

Things were different now, clearly. Twenty years had passed since the first time I had kissed Pete Killarny, and we were two very changed people. I didn't know anything about his divorce, and it was none of my business after all, but I could tell that he was a rather guarded man. That wasn't so different from who he had been as a prepubescent boy, but he had clearly changed in other ways.

And he was a father? Now that was something to get used to the thought of. I wondered if any of the other Killarny brothers were married or if they had children. There were large houses peppered across the estate, much larger than those that typical ranch hands would live in. I was left assuming that they probably belonged to the other brothers and their families. Sean Killarny had definitely taken care of his boys, and I could see how entitled Pete felt.

Of course, he thought he had a right to be in our derby,

for no reason other than the fact that they had been involved in it since it first opened. Well, that and the massive amount of money they had paid to be a part of it. While I hated to see a longtime friend of our derby out without so much as an explanation, my father hadn't given me much to go on—nothing I wanted to elaborate on with Pete, that was. Doping was something you didn't joke about or accuse with no proof. The people who didn't believe in it really didn't believe in it, and they had the law and several horse racing and animal rights organizations on their sides. But the people who did it, the ones who believed that it was something that was worthwhile and an acceptable thing to do to their animals would stop at nothing to make sure that their behavior remained a secret. I knew that it was dangerous to go around accusing a ranch of doping and even more so if the accusation had a shred of truth behind it.

And for a ranch like Killarny Estate? I looked around as I walked up the driveway through the pecan grove that slightly obscured the front of the house up on the hill. It was the largest horse ranch in the state. To accuse the largest and one of the oldest operations of doing something illegal was dangerous if it was true and idiocy if it wasn't. Besides all that, my father had no proof that I knew of. Nothing beyond his gut feeling as far as I knew. If he had really had some kind of evidence, surely he would have turned it over to the police?

The backlash we could face from other ranches was something to be considered as well, and I wondered if my father had really stopped to think about what this action could look like to some of the other ranchers that regularly participated in our derby. If we were willing to cut ties without so much as an explanation to one of our oldest associates, then what else might we do? I could see this blowing completely out of proportion if people were unaware of the doping allegations, but I wasn't going to be the one to bring that out in the open if I was not absolutely sure they were guilty of the crime. As far as I was concerned that was a matter for the police. All that we were doing was protecting the reputation and integrity of our derby. But I knew that from the outside looking in it would be difficult to distinguish that from arbitrarily deciding who could and could not participate in our derby.

I paused at the base of the hill, my keys still in my hand as I looked up at the house looming over me. I was within a few yards of the front door, and I hated that I was going to have to throw myself on the mercy of this family, but there was no way around it. And then, like all of nature and man was conspiring against me, there was a crash of thunder in the distance, and suddenly the sky opened up in a massive downpour, drenching me in seconds, and I ran for the front door.

I rang the bell for the second time that day, but this time I was soaked to the skin and knew that I must look like a drowned rat. Within a few moments, the same lady answered as before, and I could tell by the look on her face that she was already pitying me.

"Hi," I said, offering her a polite smile. "I was wondering if I could borrow your phone? I broke down about a mile from the house and..." I waved my phone in the air. "Not much service out here."

She made a 'tsk' sound and nodded, "Sure enough, honey, come in out of the rain. It really started to come down out there. It's pretty tough to get any cell service from here, but you can feel free to use our phone. There's one here in the front hall you can use. I'll just go tell Mr. Killarny

How To Love A Cowboy

because he'll want to know you had trouble. He might be able to call for a tow truck or a mechanic to come out."

"Oh, no. Please don't trouble him. I just need the number of a mechanic and..." but she had already disappeared down the hallway.

Great, now I was definitely going to have to deal with Pete Killarny again, and this time I was dripping in his grand front entry. I looked at the old-fashioned rotary style phone. It was the sort that looked like it belonged in a palace and I was sure it was there mostly for show or as a throwback to what things had been like in this house a hundred years ago. There was no phone book in sight, because after all, who had a phone book when you needed one these days, and I had no idea what number to call in town for help. In the back of my mind, I thought 911 might be the best option to get me out of here without having to deal with Pete.

"Didn't expect to see you again so soon," Pete said as he appeared from around the corner and gave me a look. I felt his eyes on my body, and I wanted to cover myself up. I was soaked to the skin, and in the air conditioned house it was freezing. I could feel my nipples hardening beneath the thin fabric of my white blouse, something that I had completely forgotten that I was wearing until that moment. Pete was likely getting an eyeful, and I was simultaneously annoyed and strangely aroused at the thought.

I straightened my back and tried to remain composed and dignified. "I didn't expect to be back here so soon, and I promise I won't take up any of your time. I just need a number for a tow service, and I'll make my way into town."

Pete shook his head. "Nah, we'll take care of you. Besides, Nolan at the place in town would take three hours to get out here at his usual rate of speed. He's good at what he does, but he's not in any particular hurry to get it done if you know what I mean."

I sighed dejectedly. "What's your suggestion then?"

"My younger brothers are pretty good under the hood. I'll let Sam and Stephen take a look when they get back." He rubbed the back of his neck and looked at me again, this time there was a little more uncertainty in his voice, and I was surprised by it, whatever brought it on. "I'm afraid you may be stuck here for the night. I mean...we could drive you into town, but I'll be honest, I don't think you want to stay in that motel. And the bed and breakfast, well, I think they book up at least weeks ahead of time with those people who like to go visit the nearby caves."

I was as excited about the prospect of spending the night here at Killarny Estate as Pete was to have me here as a guest —and that was clearly not very much at all.

"I really don't want to put you out...especially not since..."

"Since you just tried to throw me out on my ass from your derby? Yeah, karma is a bitch, isn't she?" He shook his head and smiled at me. "Maybe we can pretend that conversation didn't happen for the time being. And..." he looked around to see if anyone was near enough to hear what he was saying, "my daughter is here, and you will probably see her, so I'd appreciate it if you kept all of that talk to yourself. Between me and you, it's one thing, but I don't want any of this getting back to her. She doesn't need to know about some kind of feud between two old men. She loves her grandfather, and her grandmother meant the world to her. There is no need to tarnish that relationship."

I frowned at him, unsure of why he was bringing up Sean and Emily Killarny in the conversation, and then I remembered that I had heard of his mother's recent passing. He must have seen it register on my face.

"Yeah, and my mother was one of the most important people in her life. I don't want to make my daughter feel like there is anything to worry about or fuss over. And she's a smart one. She can figure things out pretty damn quick."

I nodded. "You don't have to worry about me bringing anything up."

He chewed his bottom lip briefly as he looked at me. "You're freezing. I don't know what we have in regard to clothes that will fit you, but I'll show you where you can take a shower and change. I'm sure there's something that will work."

Pete led me up the stairs to one of the guest rooms, but I could tell that at one point it had belonged to one of the boys when they were all younger.

"My old room," he said as if he could read my mind. "There's a bathroom over there, and it connects to another bedroom, so be sure to lock the door...although no one uses that room, so it's not as if anyone will be walking in on you." He moved to a dresser and pulled a drawer open. "There's not much to choose from, but I think you'll find something that will fit you in here. Sorry, there's not a piece of women's clothing in this house."

I laughed, and that seemed to break some of the tension between us. I also realized that I was feeling some relief at not having to worry about what was going to happen with my car. As irritated and frankly, pissed as I still was at Pete Killarny, I was sure that he would make sure things were okay. As much as I hated turning over control of my situation to someone else, I recognized that sometimes these things came along and I had to roll with the punches if I was going to survive.

Pete was standing closer to me now, and I could feel the heat radiating from his body, penetrating the wet layer of clothing that separated us. I could feel something in my core seize up, a need deep inside me awakening, and I realized just how turned on I was simply by being in this man's presence. I could smell the sweet musk of him that was like sweat and hay and morning dew, and it was all I could do to keep from falling into him.

"We'll be having dinner in about an hour. Get yourself cleaned up and make yourself comfortable and I'll see you down there in a bit."

He shut the door behind him on his way out, and I let out a long breath. Fucking hell, it had been a long time since I wanted to have someone rip my clothes off and fuck me hard, but that's what Pete Killarny was doing to me. I struggled to shake the thought from my mind as I stripped down and headed to the shower.

Dressed in an old plaid shirt and jeans that must have belonged to Pete when he was a teenager, I sat laughing at the dinner table with Pete and his daughter, Emma. She was hurrying to finish her dinner since she had a slumber party to get to at the house of a friend who lived on another nearby ranch, so she said her goodbyes early and left me there with her father.

"She's really smart and sweet," I said. "You know you're in for a world of trouble there."

Pete sighed. "Dammit, I know. I had been warned about having a daughter. You know, it's the first thing they start saying to you in the hospital. That she'll have you wrapped around her finger from the first time you see her, and that was the truth." He shook his head, and I could tell he

How To Love A Cowboy

recalled thoughts and feelings from a much different time. "I hope I have done right by her. My mother was such a help after my divorce. I really couldn't have done it without her. She had always wanted a daughter, so having that first granddaughter was a real treat for her, and I'm glad she was able to have that."

I smiled and took a sip from my wine glass. "I'm sure that brought her a lot of joy. I was really sorry to hear about her passing, Pete. It had been a long time since I saw her, but she was always very kind to me, especially after my mother and father's divorce."

He bristled and I could tell the subject of divorce was a sore one with him, so I let it slide.

"But you all seemed to have had a wonderful relationship, and I am certain it meant a lot to Emma. She won't forget that."

He cleared his throat. "You want to take a glass of wine in the other room? Nights are still a little cold, and I've got a fireplace in the study. I like to have a fire and some scotch in the evenings."

I paused. "Not a cigar though?"

He frowned and shook his head. "No way."

"Fine then," I said as I stood up. He poured me another glass of wine and showed me the way to his study, and I wondered exactly where this evening was going to lead.

5

Pete

Having a house guest was the last thing I had anticipated. The fact that it was Sara Waters was the craziest thing I had thought of in a long time and the last thing I would have considered happening. It was so surprising and unexpected, but the strangest thing of all was how much I was enjoying her company. She was good at conversation. She was smart and witty and had a great sense of humor, and that was all on top of everything else. We had grown up together, but our lives had drifted very far apart, and our paths had diverged a long time ago. It was strange to be back here now all these years later, talking about memories from back then. It was good though and I was starting to see how much I had been missing conversation with adults who weren't my brothers...if you could call my brothers adults.

But the thing hanging over our conversation as she

sipped her red wine and I polished off the last of a bottle of fifteen year Dalwhinnie, was the whole reason she had shown up at the ranch today. I knew there was more behind what she was saying, but it was clear that she wasn't ready to talk about or didn't feel at liberty to discuss whatever private conversation she and her father had had about why they didn't want a Killarny horse running in their derby this year.

Whatever Sara had to say about the matter, I knew the truth of it. It was a feud between our fathers, one that had grown even more bitter as the years had gone by, at least on the part of Ken Waters. I thought that somewhere along the way my father had given up the enmity he had felt toward his onetime best friend. He must have because he had gone on with his life as if nothing had happened, and I couldn't imagine him being able to do that if he had operated any other way. Whatever was up with Ken was his own thing, something he was carrying around with him from a time before I was born. There was nothing I could do to change the way the man felt, no matter if I thought the feelings were justified or not.

What wasn't justified though was the way he was trying to punish the entire family for something he felt toward my father. We weren't responsible for whatever still stood between these two guys, and I took personal offense that Ken Waters wasn't man enough to step up and say it himself. The truth of the matter was that had Sara not broken down in the driveway and needed help; I was already considering getting into my truck and driving the three hours to the Waters' place in Tennessee and giving Ken a piece of my mind. It was unbelievable to me that he would send Sara up here to do his dirty work and then expect us to just roll over and take his judgement like he was some overlord.

The Killarnys were the ones with the power here. We were the family who had been in Kentucky almost longer than anyone around here could remember. We were the people who had made horse racing what it was today, and Ken Waters wasn't going to take that away or tarnish our name. On the contrary, by attacking us, he was putting himself in the line of fire. If he cut us out of his derby, then he would have to answer to a lot of other ranches that considered us close friends. Ken might have viewed this all as something between himself and our family, but the truth was that when it all came out in the open, Ken was going to have to explain himself to several very important people.

One thing I knew for sure was that he didn't want to talk about the real reason behind all this. I had no idea what he had told Sara we were up to, but it was bound to be something bad since she had driven up here herself to take care of it. I knew she didn't have a clue about what went on between our father's years ago and so she couldn't possibly understand that her father's motives were questionable. I knew she trusted her father, that much was very clear. Otherwise, she wouldn't feel so compelled to do his bidding. And since I had a daughter that I loved dearly, I knew how strong that pull could be, to protect that person you loved most and make sure they stayed far from harm.

But I also knew that I could never lie to my daughter. The idea of sending Emma to do something so that I wouldn't have to wade knee deep in shit was unheard of to me and what little respect I had left for Ken Waters was dwindling fast.

I wasn't going to bring it up, but Sara was halfway through her second glass of wine. I think if she hadn't had any she never would have brought up the subject of what had called for her appearance at the ranch today, but she was a little looser now and ready to discuss things.

"Do you want to talk about why I'm here?"

I shrugged and leaned back in my chair opposite the fire. Sara was sitting on the leather sofa perpendicular to me, and she turned to face me. The way the firelight caught in her dark brown hair, now dry after her post-rainstorm shower, had made the red highlights flicker mesmerizingly. I wanted to reach out and touch the soft curls, but I didn't dare at this moment. She was so beautiful, and it was almost impossible for me to take my eyes off of her. With this thing hovering between us though, our two families could be about to go through something very messy.

"Whatever you feel like talking about, Sara. I'm up for it." I had no idea if she was going to tell me the real reason behind her visit—the reason she thought was real, that is.

She cleared her throat and set her wine glass down on the coffee table. "My father shared some information with me about what's going on here."

"Go on then."

"We don't have to go into the details of it. Frankly, I want to stay as far away from this as I can. If there is anything illegal going on around here, then I would like to have as little to do with it as possible. I just want you to understand that this isn't anything personal. We are looking out for the best interests of our family business, something I am pretty sure you can understand."

I nodded my head, but I still didn't have any clue what her father could possibly be accusing us of. "What kind of illegal activity do you think we're up to around here, Sara? I can assure you that there's nothing going on here that would make you think twice about letting us show up at your derby."

She bristled visibly at this, and I could tell she was getting ready to defend her dad again, but I stopped her.

"Listen, I know you trust your dad, and it's only natural to be on his side of things. He's your family. I understand that. And I've got a daughter, so I know what the bond is like there, but I want you to think for just one minute that maybe your father has his own personal feelings he is wrestling with. How could it be fair for him to dump this on you and ask you to come here and do whatever it is you are doing? Dumping us from your derby."

Sara looked at me without blinking. "You have got to understand that while I have my own feelings about this, I do trust my father. If he says that letting you guys go and keeping you from our derby this year is what we need to do, then I believe it."

I guffawed at that. "Really? You're just going to walk in here and tell us that we're done with you guys, after all, that time together? You won't even tell me what we're supposed to have done. Let's say whatever your father had to say about us was true. I hope you know that I'm an upstanding guy and if there was something illegal happening here then I would want to know about it so I could set things right."

That seemed to catch her off guard, and she gave me a wary look. Sara was honest, and she believed in doing the right thing. That much was as plain as the nose on my face. But it was a difficult thing to make someone disagree with a parent, especially when that person had always been on their side and had never given them any reason not to trust them in the past.

"Think about it, Sara. If you had someone at your derby who was doing things that were illegal or could do harm to someone, wouldn't you want to know who it was so you could rectify the situation?"

She nodded and pursed her lips.

"Okay then, you agree with me. We're on the same page here. I'm telling you that I don't have any clue about something illegal happening in our stable and if something is going on, I sure as hell want to know what it is and who is responsible so that I can put a stop to it."

Sara took a deep breath. "I told you I don't want to get involved in it."

"Involved in it?" I shook my head. "Are you kidding me, Sara? You're the whole damn reason the subject is even on the table. No one around here was talking about any kind of illegal activity until you came along. And I'm sure as hell not going to bring it up around any of my employees until I have an idea what it's about."

"Well, that's your business. I'm here as the messenger, and you've got the message now. I'll be leaving your check with the secretary in the morning when I leave," she said as she stood to leave the room.

"Just hold on a minute. See, there's a thing I'm not getting here. What kind of evidence does your dad have against us? I'll tell you what I know—as far as I am aware, there's nothing illegal going on here at Killarny Estate. And I know everything that goes on here now that I'm the one running the business side of the place. So if I know everything that goes on here and I don't know of anything, then your dad must have some kind of evidence that convinces him there's something happening here, right?"

Sara was silent.

"But if you won't tell me...you know what that leads me to believe?"

She shook her head indignantly and looked like she was about to head for the door.

"I think it means that you think it's me. You won't tell me

what your dad is accusing us of because you think I'm party to it. And if you're too scared to mention it then it must be pretty damn dangerous."

"I'm going to bed. Thank you for dinner," she said as she moved toward the door, but I was out of my chair and had my hand on her arm before she could get the door open. She swung at me and barely missed my cheekbone with her fist. "Let me go!"

My grip was gentle but firm. I pressed her against the door and held her there.

"You think I'm a criminal, Sara? You think that I'm the one here who is up to no good?"

I could feel her pulse quicken against my hand, and I wanted to lean in and kiss her neck, make her squirm and squeal. Her breathing was heavy and in spite of the topic of conversation, her body language was screaming that she wanted more of this. More of my hands on her skin, my breath against her ear...this woman wanted me inside of her.

"Pete..."

"Maybe I am bad," I growled in her ear and slowly let my hand glide up her arm to her breast. She was braless, and I could feel her nipple beneath my old plaid shirt. She sighed as I kneaded her breast and I nestled my thigh between her legs. She was hot, and now her eyes were closed. I wanted to pick her up, pull down those jeans, bend her over the couch and slam myself inside her.

But she would enjoy that too much, and it would be over far too quickly. I opened up the top few buttons of the shirt and pulled it open, revealing her pert breasts to me. They were gorgeous, and each of her soft pink nipples were erect. I leaned in and licked one at a time, then I let my lips settle around one and suckled it softly.

"Oh god, Pete..." she was grinding against my thigh as I continue to lap at her breasts. I could feel her reaching for my pants, but I pushed her hands away and pressed my thigh harder against her. She was so close, I could hear it in her breathing.

I wanted to hear her cry out as she peaked, but a wicked part of me wanted to make her wait. She wanted this so badly, and I could tell it was more than that—she needed to be fucked by someone who knew what he was doing. I could be that, but I wanted to make her beg for it.

I released her nipple and trailed kisses up the side of her neck, kissing her finally on her lips.

"You're beautiful," I said, and she let me lift her up and carry her up the stairs. I pushed the door open to the room that had been prepared for her, and I laid her down on the bed. She was moaning and calling out for me as I gave her one last kiss and winked. Then I turned around and left the room, closing the door behind me.

"You are a wicked bastard, Pete Killarny," she screamed out. It would take everything in my power not to go back to her room and claim what was mine. But this woman had a lesson to learn, and I was going to leave here there in that room alone, wet and wanting. She could think about me for the rest of the night if she wanted. Sure, she was probably going to be pissed, but I didn't care. She had walked into my house thinking she was going to put an end to the Killarny and Waters relationship that had spanned decades. That wasn't how it worked.

I went to my bathroom and turned on the shower, undressing and stepping into the steaming spray. Immediately my thoughts turned back to Sara where I had left her down the hall. She had been so close to orgasm that I imagined she had pressed her hands between her legs and finished what I had started. The thought of it made me harder than I already was and I wrapped my hand around my cock, pumping it several times as I thought of what it would feel like to plunge inside of Sara as she begged for me to fuck her.

It was too much, and I came quickly, gasping as I thought of her body writhing beneath mine. We would experience that together, and it would be soon. But it would be when she could no longer stand the thought of not being with me. I didn't know what this was, hell; it had been forever since I had been with a woman. Sara Waters was the next on the list though, and the girl who used to chase me around as a child would soon find out what it was like to have the tables turned. She was in my sights, and once I decided that I wanted something, I got it. There was no family feud that could keep me from getting the thing that I most wanted—Sara.

6

Sara

The twin brothers must have done some kind of magic the evening before because when I got up the next morning, my car was ready to go. I didn't bother to find anyone to say goodbye to, not after what had happened between Pete and I the night before. I had no idea who had been in the house or what they might have heard. When I slipped out the next morning, I left the check on the secretary's desk and made my way out to the SUV. It started, and I was soon on my way, off the Killarny property and out of Kentucky. Hopefully for a very long time.

My memories of the Killarny ranch had been mostly positive ones up until now, but last night had tarnished all of that. Pete Killarny was a pig and while I had at one point thought of him as a gentleman, no man of any good breeding did what he had done to me the night before. He could have fucked me and walked away, never saying another word, and that wouldn't have been half as bad as what he had done in reality. It took some serious cruelty to lead a woman on like that, make me think he was taking me to bed, only to leave me there in the bedroom sopping wet and aching.

The frustration had been too much, and after the shock had worn off, I stripped out of my clothing and tried to go to sleep. There was too much running through my mind though, and it would be hours before I was finally able to get some rest. Now I was on the road, grateful the drive was only three hours. As much as I was ready to get back to the warmth and comfort of my own bed, I knew that before a nap came, I would have to talk to my father about what had happened at the Killarny ranch and what Pete's response was. He wouldn't be happy about that, and I would be the one to face his anger about the issue.

It still plagued me that he really thought the Killarny family were doping their horses. It wasn't the most shocking thing in the horse world, but so many people frowned upon it these days, and there were many more crackdowns than there had been in years past.

Something Pete had said kept coming to mind on the drive back to Tennessee. If my father had evidence, why didn't he just take it to the authorities? If he knew something was going on then, it would only make sense for him to go and report what the Killarnys were doing so that they could be stopped. Trying to handle things himself looked shady and people were going to wonder why the Killarnys had dropped out of the derby. I knew my father wouldn't say anything about the doping, but I also knew that Pete would not hesitate to let word get out that my father had dropped him and the entire ranch unceremoniously. People would want answers, and they would be worried that the same thing could happen to them. No one would want to get involved in our derby, to register and train for it for months and months, only to be told at the last minute that they weren't going to be allowed to race. It was unheard of to do such a thing to an established stable—not to mention the Killarnys and what they stood for not only in their home state of Kentucky but in the horse racing world around the globe. People came from Saudi Arabia and Australia to purchase Killarny horses. They weren't just good thoroughbreds—they were the very best. No one would forget this slight soon.

But they might not have to. If Pete stuck to his guns, then it sounded like he would be there, permission or not. I didn't know if my father would follow through with the threat to have law enforcement there, but the threat alone scared me. Having officers escort Pete and his brothers from the event would be a spectacle, and I had a feeling that it would make waves via social media. While we didn't have network television coverage of our derby, it did stream it online, and the thing drew hundreds of thousands of viewers. People would know what had happened before the race was over and I didn't know how the Waters Derby could survive the public relations debacle that would inevitably follow.

The hours slipped by, and finally, I was arriving back at my father's house. His car was in the driveway, and I skipped doing anything else before I went to his office to confront him about everything that had gone down at the Killarny ranch. Well, within reason. He wasn't ever going to find out about anything that happened—or didn't happen—between Pete Killarny and me.

I found my father in his office, without a cigar this time, rummaging through some drawers in his ancient desk.

When he saw me, he shut the drawer and pulled the key out of it, placing it back in his pocket.

"How did the meeting go?" He asked cheerfully.

I flopped down in the chair across from him and let out a long sigh.

"Honestly, Dad, how did you expect that little meeting to go? You sent me with a huge check to tell Pete Killarny to go to hell. Needless to say, the man wasn't pleased. I wouldn't have been either if it had been me. We're ripping the rug right out from under them. I don't feel very good about it."

He coughed. "Elsie said you had car trouble or something? You stayed there?"

I nodded. "Yes, Dad. In spite of the news I had just delivered, Pete was kind enough to have his younger brothers' work on the car. I stayed for dinner, and they gave me a place to sleep and that was my day. Now I'm back here, and I would love to know what you propose to do from this point forward."

"What do you mean? You delivered the news, so it's done."

I shook my head, hardly believing that my father thought it would be that easy. "Seriously, did you think that Pete Killarny was just going to roll over and do what you asked?"

"I sure as hell do. He took the money, didn't he?"

I closed my eyes for a brief moment, trying to come to terms with the fact that my father was on a completely different plane about all of this.

"Dad, he didn't take the money, and I don't think there is any way you are going to be able to make him. I left the check there with his secretary, but I wouldn't expect it to ever be cashed. You'll probably get it back in the mail in a few days."

How To Love A Cowboy

My father chewed his bottom lip while he thought and I could see that he had been doing it a lot lately. His lower lip was chapped and cracked, and now that I looked at him I could see that it seemed he hadn't been getting enough rest. He had dark circles under his eyes.

"Well, you told them they aren't welcome here, so that will be that. There's no way they'll show up with their horses knowing they aren't going to be allowed to run."

It was almost unfathomable that he would think it would be this simple. "Have you gone over this with our attorneys? There's a good chance that there is nothing we can do to stop them from racing. It's a contract they signed with us. Whether we try to give the money back or not, that contract probably has to be dealt with in a court. I don't think we can just cancel it because we've decided it's not in our best interests to let the Killarnys race."

He shook his head. "No, I haven't called Terrence. Didn't seem like the sort of thing I should call him in for."

"But Dad, you think they are doping their horses. If they are indeed up to something, then I think you might want to get an attorney involved just to cover our asses. For the record, I really don't think that you have anything to worry about with them—Pete seemed like a pretty upstanding guy."

My father's eyes narrowed. "Don't you even think about defending him. He's the son of scum, and I guarantee you he's not much different from his father. I don't want to hear you try to defend him again."

I threw my hands up in the air. "I'm not defending him. I'm telling you what I witnessed. He looks like a guy who loves his kid and is trying to do right by her and the rest of his family. I know I didn't do a thorough search of the stable or anything like that, but dad...you know Sean Killarny. You guys were great friends for the longest time at least; I thought I remembered it that way. Now that I think about it, you haven't really been close to him in a while. Pete seems to think that there is something bad going on between the two of you, but I don't know what—"

"What did that bastard say to you?"

I thought he was going to fly out from behind his desk, but his hands gripped the edge of the mahogany, and he gritted his teeth. His entire face had gone deep red and it looked like his eyes could bug out of his head.

"Dad...I'm sorry. Just calm down. You're going to give yourself a stroke if you respond like that to something you think Pete Killarny said to me. The truth is he didn't really say anything at all. It was like he was under the impression that this was something private and he didn't think it was his business to tell me." I paused and gave my father a long look. "But you know whose business it is? Yours. If there is something going on here, then I need to know about it. I am one half of this company now, and you owe it to me not to keep things from me. I have worked hard with you ever since I came back. And I thought you trusted me."

My father bowed his head slightly and shook it. "I'm sorry, Sara. I shouldn't be taking this out on you. Honestly, it has nothing to do with you, and I wish that you wouldn't pry and ask questions. As far as I'm concerned it's in the past... all that stuff with Sean Killarny. I guess I've been thinking about it a lot more recently and I'm not sure why." He paused, then his voice took on that gruff tone when he spoke again. "But that doesn't change the fact that they don't need to be in our derby."

I sighed. I felt like I was doing nothing but sighing during our conversation, but it was absolutely unbelievable the way he was acting.

"So how do you propose we take care of this situation? The Killarny brothers are going to show up on our property in two weeks with trailers in tow, and they are going to expect to be able to race."

He shrugged. "I'll have the sheriff's department here ready to tell them to get their asses back to Kentucky."

I shook my head and slammed my hand down on his desk. "We cannot do that. Think about the scene we would be making. People will ask questions...people are going to be asking them anyway, but doing things this way would make it much worse. So unless you want to explain to fifteen other horse owners why you are sending one of the most prestigious ranches in the country home packing, then I suggest you come up with something else."

He thought for a moment. "Highway patrol then. They can be waiting for them on the road before they get here. We'll stop them."

The conversation was exasperating. "Dad, that is not an answer. They are contracted to run. You're going to have to figure something out legally. And until you do, I think we have to prepare for and expect the Killarny family to be here when the derby rolls around. Now if you'll excuse me..." I stood to leave. "I've got a lot of planning to do for the rest of the derby."

I didn't wait to see what else he had to say. The office door slammed behind me as I left. Instead of going to my own office where a lot of work awaited me, I headed outside, not quite sure of where I was going, but knowing that I needed to do something to get away from my father and whatever kind of crap he was pulling. It wasn't that I was going to clear my head...no, on the contrary, I had a lot of things to think about regarding my father and what was going on with the Killarnys. My shoes crunched against the gravel on the road that led toward our small personal stable, and I knew then that I was going to go visit Sadie.

My horse was waiting for me in her stall and just as happy as she always was to see me. I saddled her and brought her out of the stable, climbing on and taking her for a ride out in the back pasture. While most of our land was devoted to the derby and usually all I saw was the paddock and the track, out in the back of the property was where I had grown up, riding horses. Our first house, the one my parents had moved into when they married, the one they lived in when I was born, was out here nestled in a grove of pecan trees. It was rented to one of our employees now, and I rode past the place, taking in the scene of the tiny white house and thinking about all of the memories I had there.

They were few if I was honest because all of those memories had come to an end when my parents decided to divorce. I was only five years old when it happened, so none of it had made any sense to me. All I knew was that my mother would be moving to a different house and that I would split time between the two places.

But before all that, before the split, we had been very happy. At least things had been from my side of things. I had no idea what my parents' relationship had been like because I had been so young when it happened. Those memories of warmth and happiness were what came flooding back as I looked at the old house. It was those thoughts that made me think about how much I wanted something like that for myself. I had thought I had found it with Dalton, but that had come to a swift and painful end.

The end of one relationship didn't take away my needs and wants though. I still believed in love, though I had a hell of a time trusting a man after what had happened to me. I believed in marriage, even though my example hadn't been a great one. And I wanted to have children—with someone I loved and who wanted them with me. It was a dream that had been there for a very long time, and it wasn't going away. I loved kids, and I wanted them in my life. Now that I was 30, it wasn't that time was ticking, but I knew I needed to put myself back out there if I was ever going to get the opportunity to start a family of my own.

I sighed as I rode away from the house. My parents' divorce had been a difficult adjustment, but something I was able to cope with over the years. I was still close to my mother, and we had a wonderful relationship, but because of my work with the derby, I saw more of my father these days.

That brought my mind back to him as I continued on through the pasture on Sadie's back. She was clearly enjoying the ride, and I made a mental note to get out here more often with her. Horse riding had been such a big part of my life, and I wished I hadn't let it slip to the back burner.

I could tell there was something more behind what was going on between my father and the Killarnys. Pete had alluded to something but wasn't willing to go into it, and I thought it was probably out of respect for my father. It made sense that if my father had a problem that he should be the one to tell me about it. Something about the doping claim just didn't check out. When I had looked into the files, there was nothing on the Killarny horse's that would make me think they were doping. Of course, we didn't have any records on them for the past couple of years since they hadn't run the horse in the two years prior. I knew enough gossip around the derby circuit to know that things weren't great financially at Killarny Estate and really hadn't been since Emily Killarny's death a few years before. This would be the first year they had a horse in our derby since her death. They needed the money a win in our derby would bring—I knew it, and so did my father. So, of course, it made sense that Pete was refusing to back down. They had too much time and training invested in the horse they were planning to bring to the derby.

As I made my way back to the stable, I was becoming more resolved. I was going to have to get to the bottom of this, but there weren't many places where the answers could be hiding. There also weren't many people I could ask about what was going on between my father and Sean Killarny. Pete would have been my best bet, but I was in no mood to call him up and try to beg for the information, not after the previous night. A part of me hoped they wouldn't show up to the derby so that I would never have to lay eyes on him again. The thought of facing him after that hot encounter in his study was mortifying. And arousing as hell.

I gritted my teeth as I hopped down off Sadie and led her back to her stall. I gave her a good brushing and gave her some fresh hay. She was as happy as a clam, and that made me smile.

"I'll be back to see you again soon," I said as I patted her and closed the stall door behind me.

Heading off in the direction of the house, I wanted to avoid my father, but I knew that I was going to have to get into his office soon. I didn't know where to start, but I knew there was something lurking there for me to find. Somewhere there had to be some information about why he was so dead set on keeping the Killarny family away from our derby, and I was going to have to be the one to find out what it was.

7

Pete

It had been no surprise to wake up and find that Sara had already left. She was used to derby life, and any kind of business that involved animals tended to create early risers. She must have been up, and out of the house before dawn, I thought as I looked out the window and saw that her car was no longer where Sam and Stephen had parked it the night before after they were able to bring it back to life.

I showered and got dressed, trying not to let my mind dwell on Sara Waters for any longer than absolutely necessary. I knew I would see her again in two weeks when we showed up for the derby, with or without the approval of Ken Waters, but until then I needed to focus on the things that had to happen around the ranch to make going to the derby possible. We needed to know how many trailers we were taking, the number of personnel that would be going with us, and Alex was going to have to decide for certain which horse was going to run.

Downstairs, I started breakfast, and as I was finishing up scrambling some eggs, Emma came bounding through the door.

"Back already?" I asked.

She nodded and dropped her bag on the floor. "Yeah, Dani and her mom had somewhere to be this morning, so they dropped me off on the way there." She grabbed a piece of bacon and sat down at the table. "Where's Sara?"

I looked at her a little surprised. "Oh, uh...she had to leave. She had to get back to the derby. Lots of work to do leading up to the big event. And you know it wasn't in the plan for her to stay here in the first place. That just happened because her car broke down. She was ready to be on her way home, I'm sure."

Emma got up and grabbed a glass from the cupboard then reached for the orange juice from the fridge. "Want any?" she asked as she poured herself a glass.

"No, I think I'll just have coffee, thanks."

She put the juice back and took a seat again. I could feel her eyes on me as I made us each a plate of scrambled eggs, bacon, and fruit. When I set the plate in front of her, I could see that the wheels were turning in her brain.

"What's going on with you?" I asked, genuinely curious about what was going on in her mind.

"I was just wondering when you were going to ask her out on a date," she said without a pause.

I was taken aback but tried not to let it show. "Why would you think I was going to do that?"

She smiled. "See...you didn't say you weren't going to!"

I narrowed my eyes at her as I took a bite of scrambled

eggs. She dug into her breakfast as well, and I waited until she had a full mouth before I spoke again.

"I didn't say that, but...well, what would you think if I did?"

She shrugged as she finished swallowing a bite. "I don't know why you don't date. You've never ever brought anyone home. I mean...Dad, I know that you've been on dates, but I don't think you've been on any in a long time. And you've never told me about them."

I nodded. "Well, you know it's a grown up thing, and relationships can be complicated. I've never wanted to get you involved unless I knew it was someone who was going to stick around..." I realized the words only after they had left my mouth.

Emma frowned. "You mean someone who isn't like Mom?"

I sighed. It had always been important to me to never say anything disparaging about Kelly in front of Emma. If the woman ever acted like she wanted to have a relationship with our daughter, then I wanted the door to be open to the possibility. There was no need for me to share my opinion of the woman and the way she had abandoned both of us. It had never really mattered to me what Kelly thought about me or what kind of communication she wanted us to have, but I had always wanted her to have something with Emma. The fact that she had never been consistent and had hardly ever reached out over the years had been painful for me to witness, but I knew that it had to be so much more than that for my daughter who was missing out on having a mother in her life entirely.

"If I was going to bring someone around, I would want to make sure that it was the sort of woman that I thought would be a great role model for you. Someone who had some drive and knew what she wanted out of life. And I would hope that what she wanted would include the both of us. We're a package deal, you and me. You know that, right?"

She nodded and smiled. Emma was still a young girl at twelve, but I was already starting to see a glimpse of the woman she was going to be and it was both exciting and terrifying. I knew that my daughter was strong, capable, and intelligent, and whenever I decided that I was going to date again, with serious intentions, I wanted it to be someone that she could look up to.

"I know, Dad. But for that to happen you're going to have to actually go out on dates."

"From the mouths of babes," I said as I looked down toward my plate. "Okay, well now that I know that you want me to go on dates, maybe I can take it a little more seriously. I just want you to know that no matter who comes into my life, you come first. No matter what, I want you to be able to come talk to me and tell me what you think about things. This is early days still and who knows—I might not even find anyone. Maybe I'll be a bachelor for the rest of my life."

Emma wrinkled her nose. "Eww. Dad, no. You're too young for that. You need to get out there and find someone. And I thought that Sara was really nice. She's funny, and she seems like she is really smart. And both of you work with horses. It sounds like it could be a good match."

"What do you know about good matches?" I asked as I gave her a look.

"Dad, I watch TV and movies. It's not that difficult to figure out."

I just smiled and shook my head and continued eating my breakfast. I wasn't sure what I thought about my twelve year old talking about good matches, but I had to admit that she was probably right. Me hanging my hat up and not going out and dating for the last few years hadn't been the greatest idea, not if I ever intended to get back out there.

We finished eating breakfast while Emma told me about her slumber party and her plans with her friends throughout the spring. It sounded like they were going to be pretty busy before the summer got started. Once Emma had finished breakfast she bounded away off to the stables for her morning ride with Saoirse and cleaned up the dishes, my mind returning to dating and the prospect of starting all that again.

Sara Waters though—that was another story. She was something entirely different. The attraction between us was palpable, and I wanted her—badly. I wasn't sure if she was someone I would want to date long term because I really didn't know the woman beyond the interaction we had had the day before and that had been fairly intense. Before that, we had only known each other as children, so there was a gulf between who we were then and who we were now. But I was willing to find out more about Sara, and I planned to get much more familiar with her soon.

*D*erby preparation continued at Killarny Estate and all of my brothers stuck to their individual tasks to get us ready to take our horses down to Tennessee. It was one of our biggest events of the year, and since we hadn't been in the Waters Derby for the past two years since my mother's death, this was a big one for us.

Going to the Waters Derby had always been a family affair. We would all load up in our trailers and head down to Tennessee for the week. There was an area for all the people with horses in the derby to park their trailers and RVs and it was like one big family reunion with some healthy competition thrown in for that entire week leading up to the race.

I hadn't been to the derby in years though. My work had been primarily back here at the ranch and with Emma so young I had always kept close by, instead of hauling her down to the derby. It was strange, now that I thought about it, because we had gone to a lot of the derbies that were closer by, but I knew what it was all about when it came down to it. I didn't want to see Ken Waters and if not going to his derby accomplished that, then that's what I would do. I knew that what was between my father and Ken Waters was just that—between the two of them. But I couldn't get the bad taste in my mouth to go away about the man. I despised him, and I never wanted to see him again.

Because I had stayed away it had been years since I had seen either him or his daughter, Sara. And now that's all I could think about as I went over some of the paperwork that needed to be finalized before we closed up shop for the week and headed to the derby. Sara and her beautiful face and amazing body. God, how I had wanted her there in my study when she had been stranded at the ranch. I could have had her, too, but that wasn't the right time. I don't know what had come over me, but I didn't want it to happen right there. Maybe it was because I wanted to punish her for what she and her father were trying to do to us. Or maybe it was something deeper than that. I didn't often dive into my subconscious that way, but I wondered if I was holding myself back from Sara because I thought there might be more...or at least the potential.

But it was so early. Far too early to start thinking about things like that. I brushed the thoughts aside and picked up the stack of notes my secretary had left for me. Somewhere in the middle, there was a phone message from Sara buried amongst the others. It simply read:

"Bring your horse to the derby. I'm trying to work something out."

I looked at the words over and over. Bring your horse to the derby. We were going to do it anyway, but getting the note from Sara was the kind of bolstering I needed. While I was ready to pack up and leave for the derby no matter what happened, it felt good to know that in some way Sara was trying to figure things out and would try to keep her father from causing a big problem for us. At least this way I could be fairly certain that when I arrived there wouldn't be police waiting to escort us away.

I picked up the phone to dial my father in Costa Rica. He answered after the third ring and the line was a little fuzzy, but he seemed happy to hear from me.

"How are things going down there, Dad?"

He laughed, and I was happy to hear things were good. "Great, great. Just whipping up a pitcher of drinks for a party later. Is everything going okay back there?"

My father was always asking about the ranch now, but in the early days when he decided to go to Costa Rica, I felt like there was a level of avoidance. The man had lost the woman he had spent over half of his life with, and he was still coming to terms with what life would look like without her in it. After a couple of years of struggling to make things work here at the ranch without her, he decided it was better if he turned the ranch over to my brothers and myself to run. It was a single trip to Costa Rica that had changed his mind about everything. He had gone down there to clear his mind and instead he had found the sort of happiness he was looking for. While we all missed having him and his expertise around the ranch, I knew that he was doing the best thing for himself and he deserved that much. Besides, if there were ever any real issue, he would be back up here in a heartbeat to make sure everything was taken care of.

"Things are good now," I gnawed on my bottom lip as I pondered whether or not to mention anything about Ken Waters and the drama surrounding the derby. If I didn't say anything and something did happen, it would most certainly make it back to my dad, and I knew it was better to get it out of the way now. "Well, things are better now. It was hit or miss there for a minute. Had a bit of a run in with Ken Waters."

My father went silent for a moment on the other end of the line. "What's the problem? Do I need to come up there? Do I need to call him?"

"No, no. I think it's all sorted. And it was less of a run in with Ken as it was with his daughter. He sent Sara to deliver a message instead of coming himself."

I could sense my father's disappointment in his onetime best friend. "What the hell was he thinking? And what was the message about?"

I didn't soften the words. "He told us we couldn't run in the derby. Tried to give us the registration money back."

"Are you kidding me?"

"Nope," I said, and I was glad I was telling him now because he would have been furious to find out later.

"What's his reasoning behind all this?"

I shook my head and sighed. "I think we both know the real reason for it all, but I'm not sure what he's told, Sara. What I do know is that she doesn't have a clue about the truth. Her father has sold her some pack of lies about us being involved in something illegal. I don't know what...not that it matters, because none of it is true. But I thought for a moment she believed it."

"Hmm," my father muttered on the other line. "Sara is a really remarkable young woman. I would give her some credit if I were you. She is probably just following orders from her father, and I'm sure that up to this point he has never given her any reason not to trust him."

"That may be the case; I just don't know what she will think if she finds out...you know."

My father sighed. "Pete, whatever she finds, if she finds anything, well...that's between her and her father. I think you did right not to say anything. Ken is handling this poorly, and I'm afraid that he's the one who will end up in hot water over it. At least with his daughter. She wouldn't even be curious about anything if her father wasn't so goddamn underhanded about all of it."

I nodded and looked at the stack of papers I needed to get to. "Okay, well, I just wanted to give you a heads up. We'll be leaving in a week for the derby. Wasn't sure if you were thinking about coming up for it?"

"Nah, not for Ken's derby. He clearly doesn't want to see me, so we'll leave it at that. Let me know how things go."

"Bye, Dad," I said as I hung up the phone and got back to work preparing for the big day.

The time passed by quickly and before I knew it the day had arrived and we were on the road to the derby. Emma and I were in one of the trucks, hauling a trailer behind us. We were the last in the caravan of vehicles traveling from Killarny Estate, and I was glad for the time with my daughter. She was a chatter box as always and had lots of questions about this particular derby since she had never been to it before.

"It's a pretty big deal," I said. "And the prize for this one is huge. It would be great for the ranch if we could win it."

Emma chewed her lip. "Do we need money?"

"Oh...damn." I regretted my word choice. "No, it's nothing like that. Well, everybody needs money, sweetheart. But it's not like we're destitute or anything like that. It's just that things happen, the market changes, and sometimes you have good years while others are not as good. You know how things got after grandma passed away? Your grandad was really sad, and our focus wasn't really on the business at the time. It's normal for that kind of thing to happen when you experience trauma. But now things are back on track, and we're doing well. It would be great for the ranch if we win the race not only for the money. It promotes us quite a bit and helps us get a little more prestige."

Emma nodded and seemed to understand, but at this point, she was tired of talking to her old man. She picked up a book and turned her attention there, and the rest of the drive to the derby was pretty quiet.

When we arrived, I found myself holding my breath, waiting to see if anything unexpected was going to happen when we arrived at the front gate. There was an attendant there checking people's credentials and letting trucks and horse trailers in one by one. I breathed a sigh of relief as the first of the Killarny trailers pulled across the cattle guard and headed up to the area where the ranchers parked for the week.

When it came to my turn, I held out my ID, and our registration information and the attendant, a young woman in her twenties gave me a second look. Maybe Emma was right; I was still young. But I probably shouldn't be trying to pick up young women here at the derby. Not with Sara so close by. I still had my sights set on her, and I needed to give that a good college try. The young woman smiled and let us through, but I noticed her make a call on her walkie as we passed over the cattle guard with a rumble.

I parked, and Emma hopped out, immediately running to find one of her friends from another ranch.

"Don't go too far...call and check in every once in a while!" I called after her, but I knew she was safe here amongst friends...and rivals.

I started to unhitch the trailer and secure it to its place on the ground. This would be our little home for the next week, and it was just big enough for Emma and myself, though I had a feeling she would spend a few nights with her friends in their family's massive RVs.

"Hey, stranger." I heard the voice come from behind me and I turned to find Sara standing there, a smirk on her face. Well, at least it wasn't a boot to my shin after the way we had left things.

"Howdy," I said as I finished up the task at hand before turning to give her my full attention.

"You didn't have any trouble getting in?" she asked.

I shook my head. "No, I suppose I have you to thank for that." I smiled. "Thanks. What did you do?"

Sara cleared her throat. "Well, let's be perfectly clear. My father still says you aren't racing and he may be trying to pull something with the contract. I know he's contacted our attorney. But as of right now you are still on the list to race, and I want you all to approach it that way."

I ducked my head a little and shook it in dismay. "I haven't even said anything to most of the guys. Didn't want to get it in their head that it might not happen. That can mess with 'em, you know." I looked back up at her, and I could see that she was looking a little emotional. "Sara, I'm really disappointed in your father. He has no right in the world to attack us like this."

She approached me quietly and placed her hand on my arm. "Pete...I know he doesn't. I still don't know what's going on with him, but I promise you I am going to find out. I just hope that we can move forward and be friendly about things. Start fresh."

I gave her a curious look. "You want to be friends?" Friends were the last thing I wanted to be with this woman. I wanted to scoop her up in my arms that very second and take her into the trailer where I could ride her until she screamed my name over and over again.

She nodded. "I think that would be best. It makes more sense that way and is a little less...dramatic. I hope you understand."

"It felt like you wanted to be more than friends the other night," I said quietly, but with an edge in my voice.

She stared me down. "You are one to talk, Pete Killarny. You really know how to treat a woman."

And with that, she stomped off, and I was left standing, regretting that I hadn't fucked her against the wall the first chance I had.

8

Sara

The annual first night cocktail party to kick off the start of the derby had gone off without a hitch in the ballroom of our estate. It was the one time every year when I looked at the monstrosity of a room and its cavernous shape and thought that it was worth the money my father had spent to build it. Of course when I was younger I had been enamored with it and liked to act out any dance scene from a movie inside there, specifically The Sound of Music and The King and I. But I was older now and aware enough of how the world worked to think that the whole thing was a little too ostentatious.

But on nights like tonight, my goodness, was it ever worth it. The whole place had been glowing like little fireflies dancing everywhere, and everyone was looking great in their finest for the cocktail hour. I had escaped from the grownups for a moment to find the area that was set up for the kids of our visiting ranches. There was a bouncy castle and some kind of obstacle course, plus hot dogs and hamburgers and all kinds of games that the kids enjoyed. I saw Emma out there, one of the older kids, and could see that she was making fast friends with the girls her age.

Pete had been more elusive, but I had caught glimpses of him throughout the evening as he chatted with other ranch owners and people who were there to participate in the derby. He was dressed in a nice suit jacket and jeans that fit him perfectly but he hadn't bothered with the tie, or if he had it was already removed, and the top two buttons of his shirt were undone. He looked incredibly handsome, and I always regretted that we could only be friends. He carried himself with confidence that made him even more attractive, and I felt myself feeling just as gooey around him now as I had when I was ten years old. No matter how much I tried, we never made eye contact the entire evening, and I found that bothered me—it was like he was avoiding me altogether.

You did tell him you just wanted to be friends; I thought to myself as I walked out onto the back patio. It was quieter out here since most of the party was still in the ballroom or out on the front lawn where a few tents were set up. Out here by the pool, there was only the faint hint of a large party going on, and even that was beginning to die down with the late hour. Everything was taken care of, and the knowledge that the burden of another derby was off of my shoulders and under way carried with it a kind of freedom that I relished. I had done all that I could do, and now all that was left was to make sure the day to day events went along as scheduled. The rest I could enjoy like a spectator.

I kicked off my heels and left them there on the back porch and started off down the dirt road. I wasn't sure what compelled me, but the cool dirt on my weary feet felt good, and I was grateful that there was one road left on the property that wasn't graveled or paved.

In the distance, I could see the old barn, and I decided that would be a nice enough place to walk to in the moonlight. It was a glorious night. With the moon almost full the place was lit up with a heavenly glow. I couldn't have planned a better party, and I was appreciative of mother nature's little gift.

I entered the old barn and found that through the cracks in some of the boards there was enough moonlight streaming through to light the place. Besides that, I didn't want to switch on the light and attract any stragglers from the party over to the place. No, I wanted some time to myself.

Even though I had been looking through my father's documents in the file room for days now, I still hadn't found anything to suggest that what he warned me about the Killarnys was true. He had gone ahead and contacted our attorney and was working to get the contract nullified in time for the derby race in a few days, but I had my doubts about whether or not the Killarny horse would be allowed to run in the end. It would all depend on what my father and his attorney were able to accomplish, and I knew that my father had the best guy around.

I hadn't given up looking though. Still, I had no idea what I was looking for, and that was proving to be a big part of the problem.

There was some rustling behind me, and I turned, surprised, expecting to see a rat or a possum huddled in the corner of the barn. Instead, I was met with a shadowy figure in the doorway.

"Hey, Sara."

It was Pete Killarny.

"Oh, hi. I thought you were a possum or something."

He laughed. "Well, that's one I've never been called before."

I shook my head, "We've been working on this place, and I'd hate to think that the new floor we paid for in here wasn't keeping the possums out."

Pete moved a little closer and looked around. It was difficult to make out much, but the moonlight provided enough light to see by.

"This place sure looks different from the last time I saw it," he said as his gaze landed back on me.

"When was the last time you were here?"

"Honestly," he said as he scratched his chin, "I don't think I've been in this barn since you kissed me here when you were about this tall." He held out his hand to show how tall I had been at ten and he wasn't wrong.

"I was taller than you then," I said with a smirk.

He grinned. "I think you hit your stride a little early. I caught up with you in the end…and surpassed you by a bit."

Pete had indeed. He stood somewhere around 6 feet tall, while I still hovered around 5 and a half feet.

"I peaked early," I said and laughed.

"Nah," Pete said as he shook his head and turned to face me. "I think I'm looking at pretty peak Sara right now."

I cleared my throat. "You know how to flatter a woman."

"It's the truth. You're as beautiful as you have ever been and I know you said that we could only be friends…but I don't want to be friends with you, Sara. Not now, not ever."

I frowned. "You don't have to take that kind of attitude."

He reached out and took my hand gently, pulling me toward him.

"The things I want to do to you aren't things I do with friends."

I felt a shiver race down my spine and back up again. In a flash, I was in his arms, and I wasn't even sure how I got there, only that I didn't want to leave. His mouth urgently sought mine, and he explored me delicately, his tongue waltzing around mine as he wrapped his arms tightly around me and pulled me in tighter.

Pete was grinding his thigh between my legs again, and I knew it wasn't going to be long before I started to come. Just the scent of him was enough to arouse me. With all the other sensations combined, I felt like I was a balloon about to pop. His hands feathered over my nipples and I felt them grow hard like tiny pebbles. I wanted his lips around them again, sucking and caressing the sensitive tips.

"God, I want you so much," he said with a gasp.

I pulled back and took him by the hand, leading him to the far end of the barn and to the staircase that led to the second floor. It was a hay loft up there, but we were converting the whole place, and it was the perfect spot for some privacy. We went up the staircase, and the open loft doors let in the light of the almost full moon. No one would find us here. There was still some hay left on the floor, and I said a silent prayer that there weren't any mice nesting in it as I pulled him down to the floor with me.

He took his time, and it drove me crazy. With his hands, he explored every inch of me over my cocktail dress when all I wanted was for him to rip it off me and caress my naked body. Soon enough, he unzipped the dress and pulled it off, careful not to harm the fabric as he pushed it aside. I was braless underneath, and he didn't waste any time removing my panties.

"You smell incredible," he said as he dove between my

legs and ran his tongue up the length of my slit. I reached down to guide him, and within moments I was crying out as his tongue swirled around my clit. He sucked me hard, and I bucked against his face, an orgasm taking over and wracking my body. He didn't stop as he slid in two thick digits, filling me. He licked and sucked and pumped his fingers in and out until I couldn't take it any longer. I was spinning out of control until at last; I called out his name, and my body began to recover from the shuddering.

He stood up and undressed, watching me all the while. The light of the moon showed on my pale skin and I could feel his eyes on me. I returned the favor, watching him strip through hooded, sated eyes. As good as he looked in his clothes, he looked even better out of them, and as he removed his boxers, I watched as his erection sprang to life. As much as I wanted to reach up and taste him, what I wanted more at that moment was to feel him inside me.

Pete wanted the same. He was back on top of me, and I felt his rigid length against my thigh, pressing up toward my core. I wrapped my legs around him to urge him forward.

"Please, Pete. Don't make me wait. I want you now."

With that, he positioned himself and slowly entered me, each inch another level of ecstasy. Finally, when he was sheathed inside me, I let out a sigh, and he began to rock on top of me, slowly and in a rhythm that made me moan. He thrusted and with each thrust he touched a part of me that made me feel like I was going to come unglued. His cock fit perfectly inside me like it was made just for me and I could feel myself contracting around him.

I could see the level of restraint on his face. He was holding back, but I didn't want him to. I didn't know how long Pete had been alone, but I knew it was longer than I had been. He was giving me so much pleasure; I just wanted to do the same for him.

"Don't hold back," I begged him.

And he didn't. The pace of his thrusts increased, and he was soon slamming hard into me. The way his pubic bone was rubbing against my mound was bringing me close to the edge again, and I pulled myself tighter against him each time he entered me so that I could feel the sensation even more. His hips picked up their speed, and I could feel how close he was as he led me once again to the peak of my pleasure. I cried out, and almost immediately he let out a groan as he sank into me one last time, his cock twitching inside me.

He rolled to his side and pulled me toward him while he remained inside me and we lay like that for a few moments.

"I wasn't expecting that," I finally said trying to catch my breath.

"Are you having regrets?" He asked breathing heavy.

I shook my head and kissed him gently. "No, I just... didn't expect to walk to the barn and end up getting fucked in the hay loft."

He chuckled softly. "I wasn't expecting it either, but I was hoping. Sorry, it wasn't longer. It's...it's been a while."

I smiled. "I know what you mean."

He was quiet for a moment. "How long?"

"A year," I answered quietly. "We had been engaged and were about to get married. But then well, I caught him in bed with my best friend."

I felt Pete tense up. "I'm sorry about that." He was quiet again and then, "It's probably been a year or so for me. It gets to a guy."

I nodded. "It gets to a woman, too. Can I tell you something?"

"Sure," Pete said.

"I don't want to be your friend either. I don't know what's going on in your life and I know that you've got a daughter that means the world to you. I understand what that relationship is like. But...I want you to know that I'm interested if you are. And you having a child doesn't scare me."

Pete nodded and swallowed. "Good to know. I think Emma already likes what she knows about you. She was telling me I needed to ask you out on a date."

I laughed. "Oh really? So, I've got someone on my side?"

"You do. And if she was still living, you would have had my mom. She adored you, you know."

I did know, but I didn't know why. Emily Killarny had always been an angel to me whenever I was around her and her boys. I thought it might have been because I didn't have a mother around a lot of the time and she might have felt sorry for me.

"That's really nice of you to say. Your mother was a wonderful woman, Pete."

"She really was."

We were quiet for a while, just holding each other as the spring breeze blew through the loft doors.

"It's getting a little chilly, and I might need to get back so that my dad doesn't look for me. There's no telling what sort of last minute thing he needs me to take care of before tomorrow." I kissed him once more before I got up to put myself back together. "And I want you to know; I'm still trying to figure things out. I'm going to do it. You guys are going to race if it's the last thing I do."

How To Love A Cowboy

I picked up my shoes from where I had left them on the porch. The heavy oak doors closed behind me as I entered the home I had lived in since my father had it built after the divorce. In spite of the trauma of the divorce, it had been an ideal childhood. But now I was facing a lot of questions about what had really been going on behind the scenes.

I stepped inside quietly, checking myself in the mirror of the nearest bathroom to make sure there was no hay in my hair. I was on a mission, and if I was stopped, I didn't want any questions about where I had been, what I had been doing, or who I was doing it with. The last thing my father would want to hear was that I had been for a literal roll in the hay with a Killarny.

There was something for me to find. I knew there had to be, but I had no idea what I would be looking for or where I should start. My father was secretive by nature, but I hadn't thought of him as someone who would deliberately tell a lie. We had always been so close, and it was difficult for me to think of him keeping something from me, especially something that seemed to be bothering him as much as this was.

There was only one reason he would do it — to protect me from some kind of truth he didn't want me to find out. He had to know that I would eventually. The truth always came out, especially in situations when you didn't want it to.

I opened the door to my father's office with the key he kept hidden above the door frame. It was dark other than the lamp that he always kept on behind his desk. There was one single place I could think of that I hadn't looked for any evidence of whatever was going on with the Killarnys, and this was the first opportunity I had been given to look there.

His desk. There was one drawer that he kept locked most of the time. I had always assumed that it was where he kept some valuables, but then again, he had never explicitly told me what it was for. I had caught him rummaging through it over the years, and he had been quick to close it, but I never asked what it contained. There are some questions you just don't want to ask your parents and things you don't probe about. I figured that if something was my business, he would tell me.

But now things were a little different. If he was keeping something from me or something underhanded was going on, I needed to know. I needed to know why he was so damn gung-ho about not letting the Killarny family race a horse in our derby.

I felt around the desk, trying to find somewhere I thought he might keep a key. If it was always on him, then I would be up shit creek, but suddenly I had a thought. There was a brass duck paperweight that he kept on the desk at all times. I picked it up and turned it over.

"Sara, all those mysteries you've read over the years have paid off," I whispered to myself.

There on the underneath side of the duck was a small sliding panel. I slid it and inside there was a key. And sure enough, it fit right into the large drawer at the bottom of the desk, and the thing came open with a creak when I turned the key and pulled.

There was one file inside that was bigger than all the others, and I pulled it out first. The first sheet inside was a letter. I skimmed it enough to see that it was a letter from a woman to my father. The photo fell out and landed on the floor. I reached down to pick it up, and I thought the woman looked familiar, but it was an older photo, in black and white, of a woman who must have been in her early 20s, clad in a bathing suit, sitting poolside with a huge smile on her face.

When I turned it over and saw the name on the back, I knew exactly what this whole thing had been about.

The photo was signed, "Love, Emily."

9
―――

Pete

The knock came on the trailer door early the next morning, but after Emma had already left to go find her friends for the day. When I opened the door and found Sara there, eyes red-rimmed from crying and a frown on her face, I had no idea what to expect. She pushed past me and sat down on my couch.

"Good morning?" I said.

She took a deep breath. "Why didn't you tell me that your mother and my father were having an affair while your parents were engaged?"

So, she had found the truth. I had a feeling that somewhere in all this mess that Ken Waters had the truth of what had been going on between him and my mother all those years ago, buried away, but close enough that he could look at it whenever he wanted.

"It wasn't any of my business. I didn't want to be the one to tell you because it is equally shameful to me."

"It should be!" Sara shouted. "Your mother is the reason my parents' got a divorce!"

I shook my head. "Sara, that can't be true. It all occurred before your parents were ever married as far as I know."

She nodded. "Yeah, you are right about that, but my father never got over your mother. Ever. Down to the day she died, the man was holding a torch for her and that now…now…that's why he doesn't want you guys to race."

"I had a feeling it was about that. My father told me about it, after my mother's death. There was no way he ever would have brought it up while she was still alive. That was something she did, and she felt a lot of remorse for it. My father and your father were best friends."

"They were sleeping together, Pete. Your mother was sleeping with my father."

I sat down beside her. "I know."

"What led them to that?" Sara looked like she was in a daze.

I shrugged slightly. "The way my father explained it, it was not long after he and my mother got engaged. A few months or so. They got into a huge fight about something that he wasn't able to remember, and my mother stormed off. They were at a derby in Kentucky, and your father was there. As my mother recounted it to my father and then he told me, she ran into your father who was very kind and supportive and had apparently always loved her. I think it was one of those situations where she fell into his arms, and he caught her. Things went from there. My mother didn't come back, and my father couldn't find her again that night or the next day. It later came to light that she had gone to Tennessee with your father. She stayed at your grandparents' estate for a few weeks before she came back and apologized to my dad."

Sara just shook her head.

"I don't know how my dad did it," I said. "I mean, I'm glad he got over it or was able to work past his feelings or whatever. Otherwise, I wouldn't be here. But I don't know how he managed to forgive your father, Sara. They were the best of friends and then...that all happened. It was like your dad was okay with throwing it away. Then years later, even though they were able to work with each other from time to time, things grew a little tense again. I think it was when my mom got sick. Your dad tried to come over and talk to her, but he was in a real state, and my dad didn't want him upsetting her. He wouldn't let him in the house. It wasn't long after that my mother passed. Dad told me that he thought Ken might not take things so well as in, that he might try and do something because my father kept him from seeing her there at the end."

"He never, ever got over her, Pete. He loved her until the day she died. He married my mother knowing that he was still in love with another woman. Can you imagine how this makes me feel about him? Even when he was with my mother, it was all a lie. I am the product of a lie. You know what else I found in that drawer of letters and photos? I found my mother's statement on why she was asking for the divorce. It was because he was in love with your mother. She was still a presence, even if she was a state away and married to someone else, raising her own family."

I tried to reach for her, and she pulled away, standing up and going to the door.

"This can't happen, Pete. There's too much here. This is too much bad blood between us and I can't. You should have told me. You knew, and you should have told me."

She was crying again as she slipped out of the trailer and back toward her house. I watched her go but didn't follow. And then I saw Emma standing at the corner of the trailer, watching me with wide eyes.

"Hey, sweetheart, did you forget something?"

She nodded her head and approached the trailer, stepping inside.

"What was that about, Dad?"

"What did you hear?" I asked her. There was no way I was going to talk to her about her grandmother's indiscretions, but if she had heard enough, then she already knew.

"Honey, sometimes there are just things that even adults can't understand. There's some stuff right now that both Sara and I are having trouble wrapping our minds around."

Emma looked out the trailer window. "I think you need to go after her."

"What?" I asked as I looked at my daughter.

"Dad, I know you don't think you did anything wrong. But Sara is upset. That's pretty easy to see. So, if there is something you can do to make it better, you should. Are you going to date her?"

"I thought I might," I answered sheepishly.

"Then I think you need to follow her and tell her you are sorry. No matter what it was, even if it's not all your fault. You need to do what you can to make her feel better so that she can learn to trust you."

I shook my head as a half smile grew on my face. "Where are you picking this stuff up, kid?"

She smiled. "I told you. I watch stuff, and I read a lot. And Dad, you've got to keep in mind that I'm a young woman and I know how women's minds work."

"Oh, is that so?" I knew I had trouble on my hands with this one, but I wouldn't trade her for the world.

"Yup. And I like Sara. I don't want you to let her run away from you. Whatever has upset her is something you can help her with, isn't it?"

"Well, to be honest with you, it's a lot about her feelings. And I'm not sure I can fix her feelings."

"Did you do something that made her feel worse?"

I thought about it for the moment. Even though I stood by my belief that it was in no way my business to tell Sara about what had gone on between her father and my mother for a couple of weeks over thirty years earlier, finding out through a pile of letters and photos couldn't have been much better.

"I'll say this—I didn't do anything to make it better."

Emma came over and put her hand on my shoulder. "Dad, I think you've got to do something to make it better if you ever want Sara to speak to you again. If you want to have a chance at dating her, you're going to have to apologize."

I smiled and gave her a kiss on the forehead. "I don't know what I'm going to do with you. You're getting too smart for your own good."

I left Emma at the trailer and went to find Sara, but that proved to be a task that I wasn't up to for most of the day. There was no telling where she had run off to, and it wasn't exactly like I could go up to the front door of the big house and just ask to be allowed inside. I couldn't risk running into Ken and what might happen. I hadn't seen the man in years, and with the conversation, Sara and I had just shared there was too much on my mind. Even though I knew that my mother was a willing participant in all that had occurred over thirty years ago, it didn't change the way I felt about the man. He had done something that no one should ever do.

He had slept with his best friend's fiancée. For as long as my parents had been together at that point, they might as well have been married.

It wasn't until later in the evening, after another of the nightly events was over, that I was able to find Sara as she was saying goodbye to guests as they were leaving the house.

"Can we talk?" I asked, as I moved to stand beside her there on the porch. She kept a smile on her face and waved at some guests, but she shook her head at my question.

"Sara, we need to talk. There's something I need to say to you. Please, just give me the courtesy of a moment or two. That's all I ask."

She glared at me, but finally turned to go inside and gestured for me to follow her, her skirt swishing as she walked. She was dressed in something even finer tonight than she had been in the night before and she was breathtakingly beautiful. I thought about what she had looked like naked in the moonlight the night before. I was already aroused. I wanted her...of course, I did, but now wasn't the time to think about that.

She led me to another wing of the house, her wing as I found out.

"Well, say whatever it is you're going to say and then get out."

She was clearly in no mood to hear my apology, but I started with it anyway.

"I talked to Emma and I know you might think it's crazy, but sometimes it really helps to get some advice from a twelve year old. She knows what she is talking about a lot of the time and even though she has still got a lot left to learn about the world, the kid is quick and I'm pretty sure she is right about all of this."

Sara held her hands up expectantly. "So?"

I reached for her hands and took them in mine. "I am genuinely sorry that my omission hurt you. I thought I was doing the right thing by not telling you, but I realize that a lot of that was because I didn't want to say anything disparaging about my mother. She was a good woman, but I think we've all had our moments that we aren't proud of. I didn't want to talk about it because I was ashamed. That wasn't reason enough to keep the secret from you, not when you were working so hard to make sure we could still be in the derby. You were standing up to your father for me, and I know the kind of guts that must have taken."

I saw a tear start to creep down her face and I reached up to wipe it away. She took my hand and held it to her cheek.

"I know it's not your fault and I understand that you were just doing what you thought was right. It's all in the past, and you've known about it for some time, but I'm just learning about it now, and it's all quite a shock."

"I know," I said as I leaned in to kiss her. She didn't resist. Instead, she held onto me and kissed me hungrily. She was tearing at my clothes, and we were barely inside her bedroom before she had peeled away ever stitch of my clothing and she was out of her dress as well.

"Fuck me," she demanded, and I was all too eager to accommodate her wishes.

I leaned down and began to kiss and suckle her breasts which were bared before me. Her entire body was shivering, and she sighed deeply, the desire she felt palpable underneath my hands. I reached down between her legs and found her slick and wet, and I wanted to taste her again.

She was sweet and slightly tart, and as my tongue moved in circles around her clit, I could feel her vibrating under me, a strong orgasm building as I used my fingers to reach deep inside her, finding just the right spot and stroking her until she screamed again and again, until my lips were covered in her wetness. Only then did I sink my cock into her, fully to the hilt. She was tight and oh so wet; it took all of my restraint to keep from blasting inside her in a single stroke. She moaned and cried out underneath me, her finger rubbing her clit as I fucked her with deliberate, hard strokes.

"You're mine," I said as I stood at the edge of the bed, her ass hanging off of it as I held onto her thighs and plowed into her. I watched as she reached up with her other hand to pinch her nipples in turn and the sight of it was almost too much. "You are so fucking hot, Sara. Tell me when you want me to come." I groaned as I tried to hold back. "I am so close."

My hips were thrusting like mad, balls slapping against her ass.

"Fuck me," she cried out, and that was all it took for me to fill her up, my cum seeping out from between us where we were joined. I held my weight above her and watched her as she moaned and writhed underneath me.

"I'm going to need you to do that a few more times tonight, Pete. Promise?"

"Promise," I said as I scooped her up into my arms and kissed her deeply.

10

Sara

I woke the next morning with Pete Killarny still in my bed, his fingers between my legs and his cock prodding me in the back. I could tell what he had on his mind, and I wanted to stay and indulge him, but we had already done so much the night before that I wasn't sure I was going to be able to walk today.

And today was the day that I had a lot left to do. It was derby day, and I knew that Pete had to get back to his people.

"Hey now," I said as I swatted him away playfully. "You've got places to be and so do I."

He rolled me over and kissed me, groaning, and moving his body on top of mine.

"I do have somewhere to be," he whispered in my ear. "Deep inside that sweet pussy of yours."

I laughed and tried to push him off, but he was

showering me with kisses and caresses. Giving in for a few extra minutes, I let him travel further south, licking me and fingering me to one incredible orgasm before I insisted that I had to get in the shower.

By the time I got out, he was gone, but I found a note left tucked within some panties on my bed.

"Do not wear any of these today," it read, and I decided I could work with that. I laughed as I got dressed, wondering what else I'd learn about Pete Killarny in the coming days, but knowing that there was so much more that had to be handled today before I could start thinking about the future.

The first thing that had to be done was the last thing I wanted to do. I didn't even want to think about it, but I knew that I was the only person in the world who had a chance of stopping my father from following through with whatever his plans were today.

I finished getting ready. Done up to the nines I carryied my hat down to my father's office, where I hoped I would find him.

He was there, and like I had been a few nights before he was prowling through the same drawer.

"Dad?"

He looked up and closed the drawer, offering me a smile. "Good morning honey. I was just about to head out to take one last look at the paddock. Our attorney will be by soon, and he has all the paperwork. We'll be handing it over to the Killarnys, and that will remove them from the derby." He started to head toward the door, but I put up my hand.

"Dad, why don't you have a seat. We need to have a little chat."

"Honey, I know you think it's nothing. But we really can't have people like that around if they are involved in illegal activity."

"Dad." I stopped and stared at him until he sat down in his chair. I remained standing. "I know about Emily Killarny."

He looked perplexed. "What do you mean?"

"The drawer. I know what's in it. I'm sorry for going through your things, but I had to know what was going on here. I knew that it couldn't be what you said it was, but I wanted to find out what exactly was motivating you to keep them out of our derby."

He shook his head. "You shouldn't have gone through my things."

"I am deeply sorry for that. But I know Dad. I know about the affair, and I know that you and Mom couldn't stay married because you were still in love with Emily."

His eyes were closed for a long moment before he opened them again and blinked. "You have no idea what it was like to watch the person you loved more than anyone else in the world walk off and marry someone else."

"Really, Dad? You think I couldn't possibly understand that? Do you recall that a year ago I found my fiancé in bed with my best friend? They're getting married in two months. I think I have some clue what that might feel like. The only difference is that you slept with your best friend's almost wife. You are not the victim here so don't even play like you are. You drove Mom away."

He was quiet then.

"This stops now," I said in a commanding tone. "It all stops right here. You said Terrance is coming over with some papers today? You're going to call him and stop him."

My father frowned at me and raised his voice. "You don't call the shots around here."

"I may not, and I know that I don't have the controlling stake that you do, but dad, I swear to you, if you do not stop this, if you do not let the Killarny horse race, then I will walk out of here and have no part of this business again. You lost your wife because you were caught up in all of this jealousy shit and some silly feud. Do you want to lose your daughter as well?"

His eyes were downcast, and I waited for him to speak. Finally, in a softer tone than what I was used to hearing from my father, he said: "I'll make the call."

I slipped out into the morning sunshine and put the wide-brimmed white hat with a black bow on my head. I looked at my reflection in one of the windows to make sure it was straight; then I made my way toward the track.

Instead of sitting in the usual box where I had grown up sitting with my father, I looked for the box filled with Killarny men. There, in the middle of all the other boxes, I found them hooting and hollering, with Emma there in the middle of the group. Taking the steps carefully in my heels, I walked up toward them and was greeted by Alex.

"Well, if it isn't little Sara Waters. Not so little anymore, are you?" He said with a wink, and I rolled my eyes with a smile as I moved past him, maneuvering my hat so as not to gouge anyone's eyes out. I smiled as I approached Pete.

"Nice to see you again," I said, and a knowing glance passed between us. "And nice to see you too, Emma!" I shouted over the roar of the crowd that was really starting to build.

"You made it just in time!" Emma said.

Pete took me by the arm and pulled me close. "Is everything okay?"

I nodded, leaning in to speak close to his ear. "I talked to him, and he wasn't very happy about it, but the plan he was going to go through with has been stopped. There's not going to be an attorney, and your rider won't have any problems down there."

"What did you say?" He asked, looking at me with some surprise.

"I told him that if the Killarny horse didn't run, then he was going to be losing one very important employee—me."

Pete's eyes were wide. "Really? And what were you going to do when you left, if he called your bluff?"

"Number one, it wasn't a bluff. Number two well, I thought you might have a position I could fill at Killarny Estate."

Pete grinned and whispered in my ear, "I could think of one or two."

We turned our attention to the horses, and the crowd was going absolutely wild. The horses were off, and we all watched the Killarny horse, Clement, cheering him as he raced along, his long, quick strides rapidly advancing him to the front of the pack. It seemed to all happen in a flash and Clement crossed the finish line an entire two seconds before any other horses.

The Killarny box went wild with all the brothers whooping and shouting. I kept my composure for the most part, but couldn't help letting out a little yell.

Pete pulled me close and kissed me on the lips, then put his other arm around Emma. "Here's to another Killarny win! And here's to my favorite ladies!"

I looked over at Emma, who was wearing a particularly knowing grin for a girl of her age. I smiled and leaned in close to Pete, thankful for a second chance with the man who had been my first kiss.

WANT MORE? READ THE TEACHER & THE VIRGIN

An older man, a younger woman, an irresistible attraction.

HOW TO HOLD A COWBOY - CHAPTER ONE

Alex

I stepped out of my house that morning, breathing in the crisp air that blew across the rolling hills of this part of Kentucky and closed my eyes, savoring the moment for just a second more. There was plenty to do around the ranch today, but I wanted to take a minute more to revel in the stillness of this most remote part of the ranch.

My father knew what he was doing when he gave me land in this area of the ranch. It was no secret that I was the most hermit like of all the Killarny brothers. I just had my own way of doing things and my preference for how I lived out here. Even though I was close to each of my brothers in one way or another, I was the one who tended to prefer retiring to my own house for the evening or any time that I wanted to get away from the hustle and bustle that followed them all around. It seemed like wherever you found more than one of us gathered together it either turned into a friendly argument or a wrestling match.

It was simply that we liked to poke fun at one another. My mother had been very patient with us all, but I knew that while she was alive, we had caused her an awful lot of grief. She had tried tirelessly to keep us all out of trouble and aside from a few drunken nights spent in county lockup we had stayed out of any kind of major drama for the length of our adult lives. We had all been a worry to her, and I thought about that on occasion, how she wanted us all to be happy and how many times I had heard her pray for that.

Now my mother was gone, and things on the ranch hadn't been the same since her death. We were all moving on in our own ways, and things had changed even further when my father had decided to pick up his things and move to Puerto Rico. It hadn't been too much of a shock to me. I knew my father was struggling to get past my mother's death, and the best way for him to do it would be to get as far away from the thing that most reminded him of her -- the ranch that the two of them had made their own after the death of my grandfather.

Killarny Estate spread out across the vast expanse of green hills in this part of the state. Perfect for raising horses, my family had carved out their place in the industry over a hundred years ago and continued to raise some of the fastest and most sought after thoroughbreds in the country and all over the world. You never knew who might call the office to inquire about a Killarny horse. We had seen some princes and sheiks visiting our estate in the years when we had our most distinguished horses breeding new foals every year.

The breeding had been what my father was most passionate about and in the years when my mother was battling cancer it had taken a backseat to her health. Now that we were back to our normal state of things, at least as normal as things could be without my father and mother overseeing the operation, we were expecting more foals, and we had reached the time of the year when we would need to start checking our mares for possible pregnancy. And that was the thing on my to do list for this particular day.

I closed the door behind me and headed up the road. It was about a half mile to the main barn from my house, and I enjoyed the walk. Even though I preferred being on a horse, I didn't really see any need in building my own stables like some of my brothers had at their own homes. To me, it was nice to maintain the sense of being out away from the rest of the world. I had a lot of pasture lands around me where some of our wild horses from the Dakotas were kept, and out the back of my house was where the woods started and things became a deep, dark thicket the further in you went. That was all Killarny land as well, a portion of it that had been set aside and would never be cleared, at least as far as any of us were concerned because it provided a nice buffer between our estate and the other ranch that was the nearest to us.

Walking up the road to the barn I caught sight of my niece Emma on her horse Saoirse. It was clear that she had not seen me there when I saw what she was about to do. Emma leaned in and urged her horse on, and together they bounded over a fence -- a fence that was absolutely not intended for jumping. I knew better than to shout out because it would spook the horse, and at that point, there was no need. The two of them had already cleared the fence and Emma was patting her horse on the head, telling her what a good job she had done. I was up behind the two of them before she noticed me there.

"So, Emma. Does your dad know you're practicing your jumps back here?"

Startled, my young niece turned around to face me, her cheeks burning red and her eyes going wide.

"Uncle Alex! Oh...please don't tell dad. He'll ground me if he knows I was back here jumping."

The girl looked legitimately afraid of being told she couldn't ride her horse for a week, the same as I would have been if I had been grounded at her age. Riding horses had been life for me just like it was for Emma and I had done much wilder things than jumping fences. There was a memory of crossing a ravine that stuck out to me in particular.

"Promise me you aren't going to do it again?" I asked, trying to make my tone sound as serious as possible, but I didn't really have the paternal sternness that her dad, my oldest brother Pete, always managed to use.

"Promise. I'll wait until my lessons." She answered affirmatively.

I nodded. "Good. But if I catch you again you know I'll have to tell your dad about it." I hoped that she wouldn't take that word of caution the same way I would have at her age. That sort of thing would have meant, "Don't get caught."

She smiled and nodded at me. "Deal." Emma led her horse back around and through the pasture and I headed on my way to the barn, making a mental checklist of the things I needed to accomplish on this particular day.

I needed to give the vet a call and see when they could come out to do pregnancy checks on the mares. It was a task that we sometimes handled ourselves, but was best left to the professionals. Doc Halloran had always been the one to service our horses and check up on the wild herd out back, but he had recently retired, and there was a new vet setting up shop at his practice. He had assured everyone that the new vet was going to be able to take care of us all just the same and I took his word for it. The man had been in the business of caring for race horses longer than I had been alive...and possibly even longer than my father. He was in his 80s, and it was well past time for him to hang up his hat. I trusted that the man knew what he was up to hiring the new vet that would take over for him and continue working with all of the nearby ranches, but I knew that some of the older generation would have an issue with it. They always took issue with something new changing up what they were used to as the norm.

The barn door squeaked as I opened it and I made a note to grab some WD-40 the next time I was in town. Otherwise, it wouldn't get done. It was the sort of thing I could assign to one of the hired hands to make sure it happened, but if I left it up to one of my brothers to notice it, then it would be forever before it was taken care of. Pete was too busy with the business side of things, and I couldn't really blame the man for that. Taking care of his daughter and maintaining his new relationship was enough work for any one man. I didn't cut my younger brothers as much slack, but everyone knew that Jake was up to his own thing and the twins were always off doing as they pleased as soon as their work was done. Stephen and Sam were living up to their reputations as the youngest, and while I knew I could ask them to do something, they'd rather be off chasing tail than running errands for me. I was always the one who noticed the details and paid attention to the smallest changes around the ranch. I wasn't sure if it was a good thing or if I was slipping into my father's OCD ways since he was no longer around to monitor the day to day running of the ranch.

I grabbed the small notebook from the breast pocket of my shirt and started tallying the mares that we needed to have checked. They were spread out across the three barns, and it was going to take me a while to count which ones had been with a stallion in the past few weeks. We kept meticulous records on which mares had been with which stallions, but there had been an incident about a month ago with Nevada Rebel, one of our more cantankerous stallions, jumping a fence and getting into a group of mares before anyone could stop him. I tried to keep a close watch on that, and most of our breeding was intentional given the nature of what we did. Accidents happen though, and if any of the mares that had been in the group that Nevada Rebel had infiltrated turned out to be pregnant, then we were going to have to spring for the DNA testing once they foaled. It was pricey but a requirement for breeding purposes. No one would be willing to purchase a horse whose lineage couldn't be confirmed.

As I made my way to the second barn, my brother Jake caught up with me; saddle slung over his shoulder. He wiped the sweat from his brow, and I could see that he had already been up to some work that morning.

"Where are you headed?" I asked.

He nodded his head in the direction of the barn I was going to. "I've got a yearling in there I want to do a little work with. We've got a couple from Texas who are thinking about buying her, and I wanted to go ahead and get a little training in so they don't have so much to do with her initially. They're a little older, and I'm not sure they're up to the work the girl might require."

I nodded. "Which one?"

"Pineapple."

I took a look at my list just to make sure she wasn't on there. We kept the yearling fillies away from the stallions, but there was a possibility she had been with the group, and

I would hate to be sending a pregnant horse down to Texas unexpectedly. Glancing over the list, I saw that she wasn't there and breathed a sigh of relief.

"She's a little skittish," Jake continued. "I'm going to do a little ground work with her and try the flag. She seems to be easily spooked by moving objects, and we need to work on that before we start trying to load her in a trailer."

"Good idea," I said as I placed the notebook back in my pocket.

"What are you up to?" He asked me as he gestured toward the notebook.

"Making a list of the mares we need to have the vet check when they come to make the rounds."

"Oh right," he said with a nod. "New vet in town. I haven't been around to catch a name yet. Have you heard who Doc Halloran brought on?"

I shook my head. "Nope, haven't heard a thing. Hope he's a good one. I don't really want to go looking for another at this time of the year. We've got too much work coming up for him."

"I heard it's a woman."

I stopped in my tracks and looked at my brother. "Seriously? The doc hired a woman?"

Jake nodded affirmatively. "Surprised me, too. I think a lot of the older guys are having a problem with it...well, I mean not the looks of her I'm sure. But you know how the old ones can be. They were already a little set against having a new vet, but the talk I've heard is the fact that it's a woman has them a little unsure about the whole thing."

I wasn't as backward or old fashioned as some of the ranchers in the area, but it was no surprise to me that they were against the idea of a female vet. Sure, there were some of them in the area, and it wasn't unheard of, but the one serving the nearby ranches for the past fifty years or so had been Doc Halloran, and they were accustomed to him. Having a new veterinarian working on their horses was one thing for them to get used to, having it be a woman when many of them still had pretty archaic ideas about what a woman's role was would be another thing altogether. And Doc Halloran had struck me as someone who might have fallen into this group that would have ideas about what a woman could and could not do. What that said to me was that he had a lot of faith in the abilities of this new vet and whether she was a man or a woman didn't matter to him one iota.

"Ah, well. I guess they'll have to get over it pretty quickly or find themselves someone new. And half the vets around here are women nowadays. They'll just have to get over whatever kind of old-fashioned ideas they have."

Jake nodded. "I agree."

We parted and went about our separate tasks and after I was done putting together my list of mares I headed back to the main barn to look for a can of WD-40 for that squeaky door. The supply closet was full to the brim with all sorts of things, but I couldn't find a single can of what I needed.

"Of all the damned things to be out of," I said as I pulled out my notebook to add it to my list.

I stopped by the main house on my way to my truck. Pete was in his office working on something on his computer and barely looked up to acknowledge me.

"Need something?" He asked. I could tell he was absorbed in his work.

"I was just going to ask if you needed me to grab anything. I'm on my way into Ashland to run a few errands."

Pete stopped to think and then shook his head. "Thanks for asking though. What are you going after?"

"Just a few things we need for maintenance. And since I'm there I think I'm going to stop in and meet the new vet. I've got the count of the mares we need to have checked, and I thought I'd give her a heads up about what our needs are. Jake tells me it's a lady vet."

Pete raised an eyebrow. "That surprises me."

"Me too. But you know Doc Halloran wouldn't have hired her if she wasn't the best around. I'd like to get a look at her." I said with a grin.

"Behave yourself, please," Pete said with an almost scowl. "We do not need to find a new vet right now. If you could keep your hands to yourself and your dick in your pants that would be great."

I threw my hands up in mock surrender. "I don't know what you're talking about."

My older brother shook his head. "I know you try to act like the twins are the ones with a reputation around here, but you've got one yourself with just about every new woman that moves anywhere nearby, and I would like if we could maintain a good relationship with someone we're going to be engaging with professionally for the foreseeable future. If she sticks around half as long as Doc Halloran, then she'll be here for the rest of her life, so unless you plan on marrying this girl, I want you to keep a wide berth of her."

I laughed. "I think you're taking it a little far. We'll have to see what she looks like first."

I waved to my brother as I headed back outside and over to my truck, starting the thing and speeding down the long road that led from the highway up to the main ranch house.

The drive into town was easy and uneventful, and the street parking in front of McCall's Hardware was nearly empty. I recognized all the vehicles there, save for one of them, and they all belonged to several of the older men in town who passed their time sitting on benches just inside the hardware store, sipping coffee that Mrs. McCall made every morning for her husband and the men who stopped by for what amounted to a gossip session.

"How are you doing there, Alex?" Charlie McCall bellowed from behind the counter as I pushed open the door and stepped inside the store, my arrival announced by the tinkling of a tiny bell overhead. I thought I detected a strange twinkle in his eye, but I couldn't imagine what that would be about unless one of the old codgers on the benches had just told a dirty joke.

"Not bad, just here to grab a can of WD-40 and a roll of twine if you've got the size I'm looking for."

"Good deal, you know where everything is. Holler if you need anything."

I nodded in greeting as I passed by the gentlemen enjoying their coffee and headed down the front of the shop until I found the aisle I was looking for. The lubricants were toward the back of the store, and once I found myself in the corner, I grabbed the can I was looking for and turned to head toward the rope and twine when I ran smack dab into a head full of curly red hair that barely reached the height of my collarbone.

"Sorry about that, miss. I..." I stopped and looked at the face in front of me and tried not to let out the gasp of surprise I felt when I realized I was face to face with Madison Graston, the woman I had thought I was going to marry, for the first time in a decade.

GET A FREE BOOK!

Join my mailing list to be the first to know of new releases, free books, special prices and other author giveaways.

http://freehotcontemporary.com

ALSO BY JESSA JAMES

Bad Boy Billionaires

Lip Service

Rock Me

Lumberjacked

Baby Daddy

The Virgin Pact

The Teacher and the Virgin

His Virgin Nanny

His Dirty Virgin

Club V

Unravel

Undone

Uncover

Cowboy Romance

How to Love a Cowboy

Additional Titles

Beg Me

Valentine Ever After

ABOUT THE AUTHOR

Jessa James grew up on the East Coast but always suffered a severe case of wanderlust. She's lived in six states, had a variety of jobs and always comes back to her first true love – writing. Jessa works full time as a writer, eats too much dark chocolate, has an iced-coffee and Cheetos addiction, and can't get enough of sexy alpha males who know exactly what they want – and aren't afraid to say it. Dominant, alpha-male insta-luv is her favorite to read (and write).

Sign up HERE for Jessa's Newsletter:

http://jessajamesauthor.com/mailing-list/

www.ingramcontent.com/pod-product-compliance
Lightning Source LLC
LaVergne TN
LVHW011844060526
838200LV00054B/4156